ACK

I'm the fortun;
and patience fron ...., without
whom I could never have completed this book.

Special thanks to my esteemed friend and colleague Deion George, who graced my manuscript with an arresting cover and took on the unenviable role of drill sergeant when my motivation to write waned.

I also send profound thanks and much love to my fabulous mom, brother, daughter and cousin (Diana Plitt, Brian Plitt, Charlotte Basile and Kevin Crispo, respectively), who never cease to inspire me with their stellar accomplishments and endless encouragement.

Another special blessing is my very best friend Mary Ann Fortunato, who's known me better than anyone else since our formative days at Smith College. Without Mary Ann's inspired insights and genius for helping floundering folks feel grounded, I may never have turned in a college essay on time, let alone crafted an entire novel.

Special props, as well, to my brilliant friend and fellow novelist Debra Borchert, who's managed to rekindle the flames of the French Revolution anew in her book *Of Noble Blood, A Novel of the French Revolution*.

Finally, dearest Granny, deepest thanks for your

1

incomparable wit and that wonderful "gap year" I spent with you and Grampa in the Bahamas. You are the most fascinating and intensely droll person I've every met, and I appreciate and love you more than ever now that you've risen to the Greater Life!

PREFACE

Did the snarkiness of that "Bad Intentions" title pique your interest? If so, this book's for you.

I'm a copywriter who's toiled for years at various ad agencies, corporate behemoths and publishing/media conglomerates. After managing to survive my first job writing obituaries at a local newspaper–I was an earnest 16 at the time, when my editor accused me of sabotaging the press–I eventually segued to the digital realm. The challenge was to reign in my inner English Major's passion for the elaborately wrought, psychologically fraught prose of the 18th century (aka Jane Austen). After all, I had to figure out how to communicate for a living in the modern workplace, where subtle discernment is not exactly prized.

After managing to pull off a successful NYC career as a tech writer working the obligatory 80-hour weeks, I began to crave more from life than crafting high-voltage Hero messages. (Not that it wasn't fun while it lasted.) The other galvanizing factor was waking up one day to the horrifying realization that I'd somehow morphed into middle age.

We're not talking about the epiphany of a dewy-faced, 40-year-old here, but an actual "woman of a certain age"! (Queue shrill shrieks of horror.) I'm not even consoled when my overly generous friends laud my great bone-structure on occasion or how well-preserved I look for my age. ("For your age" is the abomination of backhanded compliments and should be banned from social discourse for all eternity!)

The truth is (and ladies, you know this already) once you pass 50, you're the invisible woman! No longer are you the audacious head-turner in plunging necklines and stiletto heels. Now you sit around sipping Shiraz with your girlfriends, breezily comparing Plantar Fasciitis attacks or your teenagers' out-of-control vaping. And, if you're really pushing the envelope, your last visit to that hella hot urologist might even come up.

Enter Tessie, my emphatically unsympathetic protagonist. She's a gorgeous, frustrated, complicated woman of a certain age (there it is again) who refuses to apologize about being pissed off. How do you cope after years of relying on your wily, vixen bonafides, only to end up nursing a narcissistic, hypochondriac of a husband, who can't get his head out of his Mensa-Society ass? You go medieval—that's how.

And so, dear readers, my book celebrates the pungent reality of being a flawed, fabulous, nasty woman, who's shrewd enough to use every tool in her arsenal to get what she wants. You may call her a bitch; I call her triumphantly human. And I'll let you in on a little secret: If she were a man, you'd elect her to Congress! (Yeah, I went there!)

A romp down the road from matrimony to murder...

without a single good intention in sight!

ᚥᚥᚥ **01** ᚥᚥᚥ
When a Man Hates a Woman

Spring, 1984

Always forgive your enemies; nothing annoys them so much.
- OSCAR WILDE (1854—1900)

Tessie luxuriated in the warm, swirling waters of the hotel Jacuzzi. She'd just taken a refreshing dip in the unheated saltwater pool, and the contrast in temperatures was delightful. Tessie was pleased with the way she filled out her new bathing suit, a cute little animal-print bikini with strategically positioned cutouts.

No one would know I'm a day over 35, she thought with relief. Confident in the sleek impression she made reclining there, she allowed a sense of delicious well-being to wash over her. Even the surrounding palm trees seemed to wave in approval as they swayed in the breeze. The Bougainvillea vines and tropical hibiscus bordering the courtyard were blooming in a riot of calypso colors. Tessie smiled brightly at the buff pool boy as he brought her another drink. Those Bahamas Mamas had to be super-fattening, but what else are vacations for?

"Would you rub some lotion on my back, Tessie? I'm starting to burn."

Reluctantly, Tessie wrenched her gaze from the pool boy, whose youthful sinew rippled when he bent over to hand the tourists their drinks, and looked at her husband sitting across from her, his legs dangling into the Jacuzzi. She felt suddenly weary as she took in his tall, gracefully aging physique with the slight softness around the waist, graying chest hair, and weathered facial features, made more patrician by a receding hairline. Something about the vulnerability of his now scrawny legs, once so toned and agile, brought up a tinge of tenderness in her, which she instinctively suppressed.

"Jeez, Garrison, you're high maintenance today! I was just starting to relax."

"Testy, Tessie," Garrison crooned, sliding into the whirlpool's bubbling waters and stepping toward his wife, playfully splashing her. He leaned forward to kiss her neck. His lips moved deliberately—sensuously—over the familiar reaches of her tanned, supple skin, tickling her in a maddening way both familiar and exciting. Tessie felt a constriction in her loins, which never failed to lighten her mood.

"You know how draining my allergies are—kept me up all night sneezing! Too much blooming around here. Oh, all right. Give me that lotion," she said with mock sternness. Laughing now, she reached over, running her fingers through her husband's damp, wavy hair. They embraced under the roiling water. Tessie glanced around the sunbaked courtyard. The other vacationers were too busy relaxing to pay much attention to a little Jacuzzi foreplay. Garrison moved his mouth up to linger over Tessie's ear. His warm, erratic breath tickled, making her squirm. Garrison caressed Tessie's thighs under the water then took firmer hold, pulling her abruptly closer. Tessie had a moment to gasp with pleasure before Garrison began plying her open lips with urgent kisses. He pressed the robust blossoming of his arousal firmly against her.

"Let's go up to the room," he whispered, his voice hoarse with passion. Before she could answer, she was startled by the sound of someone clearing his throat loudly nearby. It was the pool boy.

"Sorry to interrupt," he said in a distinctly un-apologetic tone. "My shift's almost over. May I settle your account? That is, if it's not—inconvenient."

Tessie disengaged herself from her husband's grip and quickly rallied her composure. With light-ening efficiency, she wiped her smeared lipstick, smoothed her disheveled hair, and realigned her swimsuit, which Garrison had yanked indecently askew. To the casual observer, she might as well have been flicking away a rogue sand fly.

"Don't give it another thought, Young Man," she purred, pushing Garrison away with one hand as she leaned back to grab her beach bag, which rested behind her on the Jacuzzi ledge.

"Tessie," Garrison exclaimed in disbelief! "You're paying the bill now? We were busy." Garri-son glared at his wife, and then at the pool boy, who remained expressionless except for the picturesque twitching of his muscles.

Tessie didn't answer her husband; she was too intent on getting ahold of her bag, which was just beyond her grasp. She considered asking the pool boy to get it, but opted instead to dazzle him with the limber range of her backbend, which she'd been perfecting in yoga class. A less driven woman might have turned around to secure her wallet more easily, but Tessie had worked too hard on her core muscle group to take the lazy way out. Instead, she continued straining to reach backwards. Her long hair flowed behind her like a Grecian water nymph's or Isadora Duncan's tunic (so Tessie imagined). She'd once seen a photograph of the alluring dancer in one of Garrison's coffee table books. He'd yammered on about a trailing silk scarf entangling in a sports car axle–beauty and art tragically cut short.

Tessie stretched back a little farther–her fingertips grazed the bag.

Suddenly her head snapped back with an excruciating jolt. A strangled gasp escaped Tessie's throat, as she tried to struggle to her feet. With horror, she realized that she couldn't stand; her hair was caught somehow. Panicked, she threw her head from side to side and strained with every fiber of her being, but couldn't rip free. Cold fear seeped through her, numbing her flailing limbs as she fought to keep her head above water. Still something kept pulling her under with the torque of a powerful winch. Water rushed over her fluttering eyelids, engulfing the stinging tears.

"Help!" she croaked, spitting desperately as her mouth filled up. Garrison stared down at her in slack-jawed amazement.

"Oh, God!" his wife, now mostly underwater, gurgled. Garrison just stood there like a glistening statue.

"Hey," the pool boy shrieked. "Mrs. Hand, are you OK?" With a speed that belied his beefcake build, the pool boy leapt into the water. He grabbed Tessie's head and tried to jerk it free. She burbled and sloshed in terror. The pool boy whipped a pocket knife from his Hawaiian board shorts. "Damn this old tub—I thought we fixed that motor," he muttered, as he hacked the blade through Tessie's hair, releasing it from the spinning mechanism.

He reached down and pulled Tessie, now limp as a rag doll, out of the water. As she lay, moaning and sputtering, in his arms, the pool boy squinted quizzically in Garrison's direction. "You OK, Dude?" he said under his breath. "Everything all right there?"

A gathering commotion swarmed around them,

and Garrison remained standing stock-still at the crowd's core. Hotel staff and ogling tourists rushed the Jacuzzi. As the pool boy lifted Tessie to safety, a bystander yelled, "She's alive."

A paramedic jumped into the water and threw a towel over Garrison's shivering shoulders. "This guy's in shock. Help me get him out of here," he yelled. "It's OK, Sir. Your wife's gonna be—just fine," the paramedic said soothingly, as he helped Garrison onto the courtyard.

Garrison fell into a beach chair and covered his face with his hands. His body shook as he choked down waves of muffled, bitter laughter.

02
Buddy's Lament

Summer, 1969

The branch shifted beneath Buddy as he eased forward for a better view. Peering down, he felt comforted by the intense August heat, which enveloped him like a smoldering chrysalis. He had wiled away the afternoon perched high up in his favorite tree, where he could spy conveniently on the adults milling around his parents' swimming pool. It was a solitary way to kill time, but Buddy was used to being alone.

During many a long evening spent barricaded in his bedroom against the shrill intrusion of his sisters, he'd often wonder idly when his parents would be home. He took solace in his toy action figures with their kung fu grip and enticing array of battle-ready accessories—what he wouldn't give to deploy a flame thrower in his sisters' direction!

Kerplunk! Splash! Buddy focused his attention on the pool again as a large, gelatinous man bellyflopped off the diving board. Except for the sunburn, he reminded Buddy of a giant plucked chicken.

"Frank, grab some burgers from the kitchen while you're up?" his mother, Tessie, yelled at Buddy's father from her lawn chair, where she held court with friends from the neighborhood. Frank, who'd been heading for the makeshift bar stationed on the patio, shot his wife a woeful look before dutifully trudging past the gleaming bottles of Dewars and Seagram's

VO, through the glass doors and into the kitchen.

"Jeez," his mother sneered in her best stage whisper, "do I have to spell everything out for him? If it were up to shit-for-brains, you'd all be starving!"

The blowzy ladies reclining around her tittered in response. Buddy wasn't sure what annoyed him more, his mother's deafening demands or his father's quiet compliance.

Buddy knew most of the guests who were gathered in his backyard that day. His parents threw pool parties for the same old crowd on a regular basis during the summer months. Such events were the only time they bothered going through the motions of a "normal" family. Buddy didn't have much experience with normalcy, but he knew his home life was a far cry from conventional.

The Taylors down the street, however—now *they* seemed typical in the best sense of the word! Parents who actually made the effort to wake you up for school and talk about your day when you got home. Meals served on a regular basis with everyone flocking to the dinner table. Buddy made a point of observing their large family with scientific precision whenever his friend Ricky invited him over. So alien was all this family togetherness and routine that Buddy sometimes got the uneasy feeling he was visiting a strange planet. At any moment, he half expected the good-natured Taylor clan to morph into a pack of hostile life forms like he'd seen Captain Kirk fighting off on TV. They'd lurch toward him, flailing their scarred and scaly limbs. All too soon, they'd close in completely, raking through his flesh with razor-sharp talons. The terror alone would finish him off before he could even bleed to death…

"Hey, Sport, how's the view up there?"

It took a few seconds for Buddy to wrest himself from the grisly allure of his daydream and pinpoint the source of the disembodied voice. There at the bottom of the tree stood a man flashing the winning grin of a master salesman. Upon closer inspection, however, Buddy decided that his smile was a little too off-kilter for a serious professional type. The man was listing slightly, as if swayed by random gusts of wind. *That's weird*, Buddy thought, since the sweltering day had yet to produce even the slightest breeze. Strains of Jefferson Airplane punctured the still air. Someone had turned up the radio by the pool while Grace Slick was bleating "Somebody to Love."

"You must be Buddy, Tessie's boy," the man said pleasantly, as if arboreal chats were an everyday occurrence.

"Yep, that's me," Buddy replied tentatively.

"Thought I'd sneak away and have a smoke out

here," the man said. "Take a break from all the small talk. You know how the ladies get when they're comparing notes—it's a dangerous business!" The man winked.

"Um, I-I really wouldn't know," Buddy replied reluctantly. He wasn't sure if the man actually expected a response.

"The name's Garrison, Garrison Hand," the man said smoothly, taking a long, luxuriant drag on his cigarette, then expelling the smoke with palpable relish. "So why the lofty perch? You on some kind of reconnaissance mission? Staking out the Russians?"

Buddy stifled an impulse to giggle. "Yeah, like they'd wanna invade this boring neighborhood." He snorted his contempt, hoping to sound casual, but strongly suspecting he hadn't pulled it off.

Garrison didn't appear to notice Buddy's misgivings. "You never know what motivates an enemy to infiltrate. Boring surroundings could prove the perfect cover for devious schemes."

Buddy wasn't sure what "devious" meant, but it sure sounded cool! Maybe one day he could manage to be devious.

"Speaking of boring," Garrison continued, his tone increasingly sprightly and conspiratorial. "This party desperately needs galvanizing! How about you and I join forces—come up with a plan to liven things up? What do you say, Sport?"

Buddy squirmed as a warm flush crept up his neck and enveloped his face, already sticky with sweat. He didn't feel the least bit lively, and certainly no one had ever called upon his party planning skills before. It was bad enough having to wrack his brains to figure out what "galvanizing" meant. Straining to make sense of Garrison's remarks, Buddy trawled the dank recesses of his mind until he could almost hear the remote whirring of motors. *That's it!* He suddenly pictured spark plugs igniting in the school basement where he'd taken that Small Engine Repair class last winter. Buddy was certain his over-taxed brain would implode.

With alarming fluidity, Garrison scooped up the glass he'd rested on a nearby stump. "Don't talk much, do you, Kid?" He took a gulp and smiled affably.

"Talking's OK. It's just the words that, that ruin everything." Buddy blushed again. Feeling faintly emboldened, however, he pressed on and murmured "Silly String."

"What?" Garrison asked, leaning against the tree and nearly losing his footing.

"I've got a can of Silly String," Buddy replied in the most confident tone he could muster. Besides his Batman utility belt, Silly String was the most galvanizing thing he could think of.

19

Garrison threw his head back and erupted into full-throated laughter. Buddy thought he'd never heard such an infectious—or prolonged—belly laugh.

"OK, Sport," Garrison finally managed. "I guess this isn't our day to solve the problems of the world—or this party, for that matter."

Buddy watched as Garrison turned on his heels and walked away, still chuckling and listing. He felt his chest constrict sharply, as if all the oxygen had been crushed from his small frame. Buddy was too scared to move until the strange feeling passed.

The oppressive heat intensified as the day lingered on, wringing out what was left of Buddy's energy. He succumbed to a feverish trance as he limply straddled his branch. The afternoon shadows had deepened and lengthened by the time he felt motivated enough to climb down from the tree.

Buddy wandered into his well-manicured backyard with its bright azaleas, fragrant honeysuckles and boxwoods bordering the lawn. His father was a passionate gardener and prided himself on tending their suburban plot as if it were a country estate. An exuberance of trumpet vine trailed over the archway that lead from the pool area to a small, inviting gazebo, shaded and partially hidden by hedges and a large, looming Druid of a maple tree. Buddy made his way past the pool and the now subdued revelers, who'd broken off into intimate groups and were lounging in various stages of torpor. Buddy noticed that his mother's lawn chair, draped with her tie-dyed cover-up, was vacant.

Desperately thirsty for a soda, he walked over to the cooler on the patio to grab a bottle of Coca-Cola. It was too hot to go into the house, and Buddy looked around for a shady, secluded spot where he could enjoy his cool drink. He certainly didn't want to bump into that Garrison character again any time soon. Buddy looked around furtively, but couldn't locate him.

Suddenly, a figure striding toward the further recesses of the yard caught Buddy's eye. (Everyone else had long since been immobilized by an over-abundance of sun and libations.) With a start, Buddy realized that the fast-moving figure was his dad and wondered where he was headed so quickly.

Hey, wait a minute, Buddy wondered. *Why are Mom and Dad both ditching the party?*

Buddy crept behind his father through the archway leading to the gazebo. He made sure not to be seen. (He and Frank weren't exactly prone to male bonding anyway.) By the gazebo steps, his dad stopped short, bending over to retrieve an object from the grass. Buddy saw his father gasp and his shoulders heave. The gasping gave way to an even stranger sound. To Buddy's surprise, his father was crying. Buddy snuck closer. His father was gazing at a lady's hair comb, turning it over and over in his calloused hands. From its distinctive design, a Mother-of-Pearl elephant, Buddy immediately recognized the trinket—it was his mother's.

Tessie collected elephant figurines made from exotic materials: jade, ivory, ebony, soapstone, even vines. She enshrined her collection under a gleaming glass display, which she jealously guarded from contamination. Tessie kept dust, smudges and the prying hands of children at bay with the ferocity of a Gestapo.

She also prided herself on her long, luxurious hair, which she often pulled up into thick, raven coils and secured with the very comb his father was staring at. She created her elaborate up-dos with exactitude, the same way she held dominion her house, collectibles, and family. It struck Buddy as highly unusual that she would misplace any object, let alone one she valued as much as that fancy comb.

Mesmerized by his father's weeping, Buddy was too preoccupied to remain hidden. His dad stifled his tears and turned his head in Buddy's direction. Their eyes met, but Frank looked right through his trembling son.

"Careless," Frank said, and then sighed. "When did she get to be so careless?" His voice was flat, robotic. Buddy took a step forward.

"Not now, son. I'm busy," Frank said turning away, and Buddy crept back into the gathering shadows.

⤛⤜ **03** ⤛⤜
Diminishing Returns

Fall, 2003

The cavernous data center was dimly lit by the phosphorous glow of dozens of monitors, neatly aligned in their respective workstations, most of them vacant at this early hour. The great room hummed with the processing of servers. Although Garrison had long since become accustomed to the monotonous drone of the computers, he sometimes felt enveloped by a swarm of locusts. On overnight shifts like this one—his vision blurred from poring over computer screens to diagnose system problems, his mind hazy from lack of sleep—he was especially prone to wild imaginings.

Garrison stood up and stretched expansively, squeezing his eyes shut then blinking a few times to refresh his bleary vision.

I've got to stop staring at that damn screen for hours on end, he thought. *It's petrifying my brain. Christ, I need a vacation – bring on the beach, tiki bar, scantily-clad island girls!* Garrison shook his head in a vain attempt to dislodge these distracting thoughts. *Focus, you dirty old bastard.*

Garrison was viewed as a thought leader at Beacon Communications. No one could troubleshoot a temperamental operating system or network with greater finesse. When Garrison was still an Internet Technology novice, working toward his first impor-

25

tant industry certification, his project team leader had lavishly praised him during an informal "lunch and learn" subnet masking exercise. His words had stuck with Garrison, who took refuge in mulling them over when things got dicey at work, which was often the case lately.

"Gary," his team leader had said, needling Garrison with the nickname he most despised, "your analysis is brilliant. No, brilliant's not the word. It's *elegant—fuckin' elegant*! It's a shame you're too damn lazy to bother with administrative details. In fact, if you weren't so *outrageously* sloppy managing your projects, you'd probably be running this shit hole."

The guy wasn't one to mince words, and Garrison couldn't help but give him grudging respect. Come to think of it, the praise hadn't been so lavish after all, but it was dead on—and Garrison valued intellectual rigor above all else, even given his infamous towering ego, which he knew was now crumbling like the façade of a venerable, decaying old building.

Garrison walked over to the break room to pour himself a cup of coffee, then slouched at one of the tables, hoping that the room's harsh florescent lighting would wake him up. He checked his watch: 5:30 a.m. Two and a half hours to go! Soon employees on the 6 to 3 shift would begin streaming in. He'd be swept up in the workday bustle and given a temporary reprieve from his ruminations.

Garrison had been put in charge of training the latest batch of recruits at the data center, kids just out of college or technical school. While teaching the introductory Data Networking class, he enjoyed his students' precocious irreverence and loved breaking up the monotony by quipping about the latest South Park episode or pop culture icon. He looked forward to coaching his new charges in a few minutes, after they'd dragged themselves in from a night of youthful frolics (or so Garrison imagined, judging from their habitual yawning and draped postures at the conference table).

They make such an endearing effort to look alert, Garrison thought with an avuncular chuckle. *The 6 a.m. shift is a killer if you have a social life!*

Garrison didn't have to worry about his own social life impinging on his work. He'd long since sworn off the binge drinking that had plagued his halcyon days as an undergraduate at Amherst. He remembered with nostalgia competing while barely coherent at the New England Fours regatta. His friends had deposited him on the shores of Lake Quinsigamond at dawn, where he managed to distinguish himself during the first heat of the morning. He rowed like a champion despite his skull-splitting hangover (a trifling nuisance), committing every sinew of his being to accelerate the team's strokes per minute. In his decidedly biased opinion, he'd propelled that shell with torso-wrenching intensity worthy of Ben-Hur. Later, his comrades gave him a rousing ovation just for staying conscious long enough to help ace the finals that afternoon.

Too bad I can't blame my senior moments on the booze, Garrison reflected. *It's wretched getting old!* Recently, he'd drawn a blank introducing a new recruit at the water cooler, and was taking longer than usual to solve routine binary equations. He wrote off such lapses as symptoms of stress at home, figuring some fallout was to be expected after 30 years in the marital trenches.

Garrison had met his third wife, Contessa, at the local racquet club. Still smarting from his second divorce, Garrison had turned to grueling physical exercise to dull his mental anguish. One day, while sweating it out on the courts, he observed a striking woman hitting moon balls nearby. She was a brunette—not classically beautiful so much as exuding a potent carnal allure. Her glossy profusion of hair was piled up into a stylishly disheveled bun, and her white Lacoste shirt was haphazardly buttoned, showcasing an epic crevasse of cleavage.

The woman lunged to return a drop shot, winning the point. As she turned to walk back to the baseline, she adjusted her tennis pants under her tight, short skirt. Garrison's jaw dropped, and then he aced his opponent with a scorching serve. The other men playing nearby took notice of the exotic newcomer between volleys. A ripple of titillation pulsed throughout the club.

Garrison eyed the woman with fascination as she played her way through a set. There was something exaggerated, yet organic, about her undulating stride that reminded him of Marilyn Monroe and her signature "horizontal walk." The woman continued her exertions for 45 minutes or so without marring her makeup or breaking a sweat. She then stepped delicately off the court and headed for the soda machine.

Garrison feigned a pulled hamstring and quickly excused himself from his match. He threw a towel around his shoulders and followed her with as much machismo as he could muster. He attempted to swagger, shrugging off misgivings that this show of heightened masculinity could backfire. The woman, who was sitting on a bench sipping a Tab, smiled at him as he approached. Spurred on by this acknowledgement, Garrison sat down next to her.

"You were playing on court seven," she chirped adenoidally. Garrison suppressed a cringe. "What's with the limp—sprained something with that big serve?" She snapped her gum for emphasis. *Great,* Garrison groaned silently. *She thinks I'm a gimp!*

"No, just reeling from a tough break-up," he replied without missing a beat. Since the oversexed lothario routine didn't seem to be working, he decided to play up his wounded, sensitive side. "I thought she cared, but it turns out she never really knew me," Garrison sighed dramatically. "I feel like such an idiot. Oh well—*c'est la guerre!* As the great Fitzgerald once said, 'The victor belongs to the spoils.'"

The woman gazed at Garrison sympathetically. She placed her hand over his and said with misty-eyed sincerity, "Who's Fitzgerald? One of your buddies?"

"Hey, Mr. Hand!" Garrison nearly jumped out of his chair. A rumpled looking kid had poked his head into the doorway and was waving at him from across the break room.

"Oh, hi Rudy," Garrison replied. "I guess my thoughts were a million miles away—didn't see you come in. How about some coffee?"

"Not this morning, Mr. Hand—gotta update some reports before class. I wanna get out of here on time tonight for the opening. You and Mrs. Hand are going, right?"

Rudy and Garrison were sci-fi film fanatics. During breaks at work, or while partnering during nightshifts that dragged on endlessly, they often discussed the mind-bending special effects and plot machinations of the latest cyber adventure. To the uninitiated among their friends, the intensity of this ongoing analysis was a bit scary. The two colleagues also shared a semi-hysterical obsession with *The Matrix*, which they hailed as the holy grail of its genre, and were eagerly anticipating the release of its sequel, *The Matrix Reloaded*. In the weeks building up to the movie's much-hyped opening, they channeled their mounting excitement by parsing the series' philosophical underpinnings in exhaustive detail.

Nevertheless, to Garrison's embarrassment, he couldn't say yes to Rudy's question. He knew his response wouldn't make sense to the quirky, free-spirited young man, who cared nothing for convention or the precarious politics of matrimony.

Let's just call it like it is, Garrison thought mournfully. *I'm pathetic and pussy-whipped!*

"Sadly, Rudy," he sighed, "the Missus doesn't share our keen appreciation of *The Matrix* or its existential charms. I'll have to find a less obtrusive time to go. Friday nights are devoted to wining and dining my wife."

Rudy raised his eyebrows. "Bummer, Mr. Hand. That really sucks! Well, better get going. See you in class. Morpheus rules!"

Rudy gave Garrison the "hang loose" sign, stepped out of the break room and walked toward the data center's main work area. Garrison checked his watch again. The dial was flashing 5:45—5:45—5:45. His alarm had gone off; almost time to start class. Garrison leaned into the table and pushed himself up from the chair. He braced his hands against his lower back and winced.

When did I turn into such a fossil? he thought wistfully. *One minute I was in my prime; the next, old age had wreaked havoc. I'm a complete train wreck!* Shaking his head, Garrison shuffled stiffly over to the coffee pot and fixed himself another cup. He deliberately inhaled the steaming beverage's rich aroma.

Aaaaaahhhh…the morning does have its humble consolations. Shit, now I'm spouting platitudes! I could always do commercials—retire from this techie gig and fill that casting pool shortage of silver-haired codgers! Garrison took a sip and, grinning ironically, walked out the door toward steps that climbed to the training room.

The training room seemed claustrophobic in contrast to the central work area Garrison had just left, with its vaulted ceilings and open floor plan. It occurred to Garrison as he entered the stuffy office space that its narrow confines were better suited to suffocating brain matter than fostering knowledge. He walked over to the windows spanning the length of the grey soundproofed walls and looked down several stories to the main floor, now swarming with workday activity. With a sigh, he drew the heavy blinds closed, blocking out the distracting view, along with any natural light. Garrison figured his young students would need all his help to focus on the day's mind-numbing lesson plan.

Nothing like a crack-of-dawn lecture on Internet protocols, Garrison thought. *I need to keep these poor kids from lapsing into a collective coma!*

Garrison turned to the white board at the head of the conference table and, while his students straggled in, busied himself with diagramming various network trafficking scenarios. He was intimately familiar with the topographies he sketched, having worked with them for years, and drew quickly with staccato flourishes of the marker. Upon completing his last drawing, he wiped his hands and turned to greet the new recruits, now fully assembled. "So, how's everyone doing this morning?"

"The class muttered a jumbled response, "Good. Like crap! Not bad. Stellar!" Garrison smiled at that last reply—typical Rudy, the eternal optimist!"

"Great, then you're ready for a little TCP/IP," Garrison said archly, flashing his best Jack Nicholson grin. "Let's get down to it, shall we?" He pointed to the white board with a sweeping gesture. "So which of these drawings shows the ATM mode, and what are the scalability issues for this type of network?"

Garrison coaxed the class into participating by peppering his technical comments with wry banter. He was beginning to think he'd salvaged the morning from a quagmire of tedium and even indulged in a little self-congratulation. *They actually seem interested,* Garrison marveled.

Then Rudy raised his hand. "What does MPLS stand for again?" he asked. "I left my book at home."

Garrison's mouth opened automatically, ready to volley a rote answer. Yet, to his utter bewilderment, he couldn't summon up a response. The answer poised at the tip of his tongue had vanished—probably defecting to the rescue of some other old bastard struggling to stay glib and relevant. He felt like he'd stumbled into a strange vortex in reality. Surprising

34

himself, Garrison flared with frustration and fury. He felt driven to save face.

"Rudy, what happened—woke up with Clue Deficit Disorder?" Garrison shot back, hoping that Rudy would laugh in his usual good natured way and forget about his question.

"Good one, Mr. Hand. I'm actually no more clueless than usual this morning. I just can't remember what the acronym stands for, and it's driving me nuts," Rudy persisted, blithely unaware of Garrison's rising panic.

"Jesus, Rudy," Garrison sneered. "How long do you intend to pull this überfuckwit routine? It's wearing thin." The class snickered nervously.

Rudy stared at Garrison, not sure whether to laugh or cry. "Mr. Hand, what's going on?" he stammered.

Garrison steeled himself to respond. "I mean it, Rudy. You'd better start taking this job seriously, or you're out of here."

Rudy cringed. "See if I give a flyin' fuck—Mr. Hand-Job," he gasped.

As Rudy stormed out of the room, slamming the door behind him, Garrison turned to the white board and deftly drew another network diagram.

04
Conspicuous Consumption

Garrison felt out of sorts at dinner, despite the restaurant's pleasant ambiance and his wife's incessant chatter, which he usually blocked out for self-preservation. Over the years, he'd made a game of ignoring his wife's running commentary on the hottest shopping bargains or latest celebrity scandals. He'd figured out how to provide generic responses at key intervals, so she'd have no idea his mind was elsewhere.

Tonight, however, Garrison's thoughts were too scattered and disturbing to barricade him from her voice. In fact, nails raking a blackboard would have been a more pleasant accompaniment to his Chilean Sea Bass and bottle of Chardonnay.

"So, Luca finally convinced me to add layers around my face and some chunky highlights," Contessa said between ample bites. "He's such a talented stylist—and he's so busy, they've closed his appointment book to new clients. I was the last one he agreed to take on. My girlfriends are so jealous. This pasta could use more garlic. How's your fish?"

Garrison didn't answer her question, deciding instead to take an extreme measure. He badly needed to talk with someone about the day's unsettling events, and his wife—God help him—was the only someone at hand. He gulped his wine and leaned toward her.

"Tessie," he said. "Do you think I've been irritable lately?"

Her eyes widened at this unexpected detour in the conversation. "What do you mean?" she asked. "Why are you getting all serious on me? We're supposed to enjoy the evening."

As soon as the question had escaped his lips, Garrison regretted opening up to his wife, and now her response only heightened his qualms.

Sweet Jesus, Garrison thought. *I should have known better.* But his anxiety was so extreme that he soldiered on.

"I lost it with one of the guys at work today, Tessie, a really good kid—a friend, in fact—and I just don't know why." Suddenly, Garrison's eyes welled with tears, which he hoped the dim lighting would conceal.

"Yeah, and...," Contessa asked.

"I'm so confused. I insulted this poor kid and yelled at him. Christ, he's barely Buddy's age," he stammered, not sure why an image of Contessa's son by her previous marriage had surfaced.

"Geez," she hissed. "Why all the drama? It's probably just a little male menopause, and what's so terrible, anyway? I always thought you needed to grow some balls at work. They never did give you that raise."

Garrison seethed with frustration. He stared at his wife with sickening clarity. She sat there impassively and continued to eat, her appetite apparently undiminished—how could she be so oblivious to his suffering? Didn't he explain his problem vividly enough?

Is it possible she thinks I'm joking? Garrison puzzled, but he knew he was grasping at straws.

"I need some air." Garrison stood up abruptly, threw his napkin on the table, and stomped out of the restaurant. He pushed through the front door and breathed a sigh of relief at the balmy waft of ocean air against his face. As the door swung closed, the din reverberating from the restaurant's crowded confines gradually subsided. Garrison stood beneath an awning and lit a cigarette.

The small trees bordering the entranceway to the restaurant were adorned with twinkle lights, reminding Garrison of gala evenings past, idled away at art openings or the opera. His wife had always hung on his arm, arresting in her form-fitting gown and dramatic jewelry. She'd never failed to draw lascivious glances from most males in the vicinity.

She could jump start a guy without a pulse, Garrison thought, smiling sardonically. It had never fully dawned on him until this instant that he'd foregone the fulfillment of a sentient companion for the hollow pleasures of a trophy wife.

After all, Tessie had never shared his cultural interests. While quicksilver cognition was his stock-in-trade, hers was her physical appeal, especially her infamously robust cleavage, which she wielded with increasing assertiveness as she aged, like some desperate currency.

The chasm in their coupleship extended beyond a mere divergence in pastimes, however. Tessie deeply resented Garrison's ability to immerse himself in his fertile imagination. She believed that any time spent in deep thought was sorely misallocated—after all, there wasn't opportunity enough for Garrison to sufficiently admire her, satisfy her, or otherwise sate her craving for worldly trappings. It particularly irked her when he became absorbed in a hobby for days, as if under some hypnotic spell.

"You've got that Rasputin thing going again," she'd spit like a dyspeptic feline. While sitting restlessly through a TV documentary on the Russian Revolution with her husband, Contessa had been introduced to the life of Rasputin, the self-styled "holy man" who achieved ill-fated prominence by entrancing the Tsarina. Though the politics of St. Petersburg's glittering salons held little interest for Tessie, who nursed an aversion to overtly intellectual topics, she was drawn to the unwashed charms of the nefarious mystic.

"Tzar, Schmar," she'd remarked to Garrison after enduring the show. "I'll take that grungy, bulletproof monk any day."

What do I do now? thought Garrison, leaning wearily against the restaurant's shingled siding, his head starting to throb. *I've fucked up royally—30 years of marriage down the drain.*

He hung his head and sighed, bracing for an onslaught of emotions: anger, self-pity, resentment, stinging regret. The feelings never came, though; he just felt numb, except for the dull ache pervading his weary brain.

So much for personal enlightenment, he chided himself. *Even if I could fix my life, which one of my many transgressions do I tackle first? Breaking up Tessie and Frank's marriage to satisfy my selfish lust? Failing my kids? Failing her kids? Failing Rudy today?*

It was obvious to Garrison that redemption for an evening this miserable could only be found at the bottom of a bottle.

There he goes, the Dean of Drama, Contessa

thought as Garrison charged out of the restaurant. *The man thinks too much, that's his problem.*

If she'd felt like it, Contessa could have come up with a richly detailed laundry list of Garrison's shortcomings right then and there—and how she'd relish bringing each one of them to his attention. The restaurant was just too deliciously trendy, and she too pleasantly buzzed, to ruin it all by focusing on his annoying faults.

Let him stew outside for a while, Contessa thought, as she sipped her last drop of wine, signaling the waiter while deftly applying more lipstick. *It's so typical of him to wreck a perfectly good night out. His feelings get hurt more easily than a little girl's.*

Satisfied with her insightful assessment of Garrison's emotional state, Contessa sat back to survey the scene. The restaurant, aptly named "Clique," overflowed with a menagerie of characters, all frenetically energized by the place's swank panache. Contessa thanked the waiter as he refilled her glass of wine, making eye contact as she smiled indulgently.

Some well-turned-out businessmen at the next table had burst into raucous laughter, presumably over the latest boardroom battle, while a young couple at another table nearby were clutching hands, immersed in emotional conversation. The girl was crying softly without attempting to fix her mascara, which ran in muddy rivulets down her face.

The bar area was packed with denizens, most advertising their embrace of an alternative lifestyle. A cluster of clean-cut lesbians nursed their drinks and cast appraising glances at the other women pushing their way up to the bar. Contessa was surprised by how casually the lesbians dominated the room. Each sported an artfully razored haircut, a tight tank top, and crisp cargo pants, highlighting her imposing physique.

Clearly the era of the frumpy dike in Birkenstocks is over, Contessa thought. As she watched the women, she felt stirred by their aura of empowerment.

They're not sweating any man's mood swings, Tessie thought triumphantly. *Why should I bother smoothing things over with Garrison, when he'll just invent something else to worry about? If he didn't have so damn much money, I would have left him years ago.*

Whenever Tessie thought about Garrison's sizable and richly diverse portfolio, she quivered with eagerness, like a schoolgirl with a crush. She knew that, despite his fancy education, he hadn't always been rich. In his mid-30s, Garrison had become the stunned beneficiary of a handsome trust fund. His benefactor was a great aunt, whom he barely knew, but who'd had the good graces to expire and leave him a small fortune. Much to Tessie's supreme irritation, this profound improvement in Garrison's financial status hadn't served to loosen his purse strings.

To the contrary, he'd become cheaper than ever. When Garrison made a flurry of secretive investments upon the advice of his family banker, Tessie deployed her most high voltage charms in an attempt to seduce the details out of him. She tried casually questioning him in bed while striking precariously energetic Tantric poses, but no matter how many times she feverishly flexed her thighs, her exertions were fruitless. Garrison entered enthusiastically into their sex play, but refused to answer her thinly veiled questions regarding the state of his coffers.

Oddly enough, this core tension between them kept their relationship strained but vital, since Tessie could never admit to a chink in her arsenal of feminine wiles. Over the years, she kept advancing on Garrison like a one-woman phalanx, spurred on by frustration that continued to smolder in her vitals. She couldn't be sure if Garrison planned to leave her all that money which, naturally, she felt she richly deserved. Tessie had a sneaking suspicion that he intended, instead, to leave his millions to his two daughters by his second wife (to whom Tessie dismissively referred as "that frigid bitch").

Tessie loathed Garrison's daughters, who had both joined the Peace Corps and later busied themselves with furthering the greater collective good. They hadn't spoken to their father in years, yet Tessie still smarted at the notion that her stepdaughters considered her presence in Garrison's life an intrusion and a disgrace, since the union had ripped their family apart. Still, Garrison yearned for his daughters' love and approval.

The waiter approached again to light the candle at Tessie's table and top off her glass of wine. She shot him a coy, sidelong glance, twirling her manicured fingers in the tendrils that had escaped the confines of her chignon.

"Can I interest you in some dessert, Miss?" the waiter asked, deftly scraping crumbs from the table as he reached for a dessert menu in his apron pocket.

Tessie felt herself warming to this tall, earnest young man, who addressed her in such an easy, conversational tone. *Thank God he didn't call me Ma'am,* she thought.

"I don't know," she replied playfully. "I wasn't planning to be naughty tonight, but you might be just the one to persuade me." She tossed her head back to showcase her silvery laugh and heard a distinct clatter behind her. The heavy, antique ivory comb, which secured her updo, had become dislodged and fallen to the tile floor. Her curls came uncoiled, falling about her bare shoulders in a dark profusion, iridescent in the candlelight. The waiter quickly bent over to retrieve the fallen object, just as Tessie leapt from her chair to search for it, knocking her glass off the table. She was hoping they'd collide, so she could press her ample décolletage against his pristine, white shirt, but he nimbly stepped aside, scooping up the comb and presenting it to her with a flourish.

"I believe this is yours, Miss," he said with crisp professionalism. Tessie was taken aback that the waiter hadn't played into her hands. It was usually so easy to entice young men, especially those who were paid to wait on her—but before Tessie could bend the situation to her will, she was stopped cold. Garrison was staring in at her through the window by their table, his pale face scowling with spectral intensity. Apparently, he'd been observing long enough to witness her exchange with the waiter.

"Oh, shit—this is just what I need," Tessie hissed under her breath, as she snatched her comb from the waiter and gathered her hair into a haphazard bun.

When the magnitude of his shortcomings first dawned on Garrison as he stood outside the restaurant chain smoking, he went weak at the knees. If the side of the building hadn't been there to prop him up, he might have collapsed to the ground and writhed with angst. Instead, he just slumped there against the shingles, paralyzed with depression.

My God, I've actually hit the wall—literally, he thought dejectedly. After a few minutes of intense leaning, however, his back began to itch. Garrison figured he could just as easily be abjectly miserable while mobile and began to wander mindlessly around the grounds surrounding the building.

It was a summer night to savor. The fragrance of honeysuckle and mowed grass wafted on the cool, velvety breeze. Fireflies flickered a syncopated light show over the potato field adjacent to the restaurant lot. As he strolled along, basking in the night air, Garrison felt the fog of melancholy begin to disperse. The pure smell of freshly cut lawn made him think of the long, glorious summers he'd spent as a college student, earning money by trimming hedges and tending yards for the wealthy families in town. He'd enjoyed the good, hard, honest work, which offset the intellectual rigors of the previous semester. He also remembered the girls he knew back then, who respected him enough to challenge his thinking, gazing deep into his eyes with equal curiosity and passion. His spirits plummeted again as he thought of Tessie, whose libido hinged on wanting to grasp without comprehending, to gain without investing.

Without knowing why, Garrison stopped in front of a window, which gave a clear view of the restaurant's interior. He stepped up to the luminous panes of glass and peered through. To his surprise, he saw the table at which he and Tessie had been seated earlier that evening. The candle had been lit (*I must have been out here a while,* Garrison thought with detachment), and Tessie was smiling at a handsome, young waiter, who busied himself among the tables. He was athletically built, moving with a natural grace that underscored his masculinity.

I used to carry myself with that same pride and determination, Garrison thought wistfully. *He's probably waiting tables to pay his tuition or supplement a soccer or lacrosse scholarship.* Garrison continued to observe the scene, and even managed to chuckle as he saw the waiter skillfully sidestep Tessie's advances.

She'll be in a foul mood tonight, he thought, his spirits starting to lift. Suddenly, Garrison realized that he had been blessed with the rare opportunity to watch a younger version of himself in action, striving gamely to succeed and nimbly avoiding the mistakes that he, himself, had made through sheer carelessness—or drunkenness.

I've let the best part of myself slip away, Garrison mused. *I've let Rudy down, the only one left who could see my better nature. When I betrayed his youth and innocence, I gave up on myself. This doesn't have to be the way it ends, though. I may be losing my mind, but I can still salvage my dignity and make things right—starting now.*

Just then, Tessie turned and, with a start, saw her husband. Their eyes locked. Filled with a new sense of purpose, Garrison turned on his heels and walked briskly back into the restaurant, striding up to the table where the waiter was realigning the place settings.

"Hello, Sir," the waiter said with smooth deference. "We've had a little mishap, but I'm taking care of it. Meanwhile, would you and the young lady care to sample our dessert menu?"

Garrison studied the young man silently for a moment. He was still out of breath from having sprinted back into the restaurant. Tessie sat demurely, pretending to scrutinize the dessert menu.

Garrison collected himself and spoke in a measured pace.

"No dessert for us tonight, Sport. But please accept this token of my appreciation—I can tell you've been working hard to take special care of my wife. She's high maintenance, you know—not everyone makes the grade." Garrison slipped a silver money clip, embedded with an Indian head nickel, from his back pocket. He had bought the clip with the first real money he'd ever made tending lawns so many summers ago. Garrison gave Tessie a significant look, licked his thumb ceremoniously, and then slapped five crisp $100 bills upon the linen tablecloth. Tessie blanched at the sight of the money stacked in front of her.

"Garrison!" she sputtered. The waiter stepped back in surprise. "Sir, this isn't necessary," he said.

Garrison held up his palm, gesturing the waiter to hold off. His face wreathed in a smile of ruthless altruism, he continued to peel bills off his wad of cash, not stopping until he'd laid $1,000 upon the table. Tessie's ghostly pallor morphed to a mottled purple. She rose to her feet to confront her husband. But before she could continue, she realized she had an audience. She struggled to choke down the bitter tirade welling in her throat, which had suddenly gone bone dry. The waiter, who was now clutching the wad of money to his starched uniform, beamed first at her, then at Garrison, with a look of shocked gratitude. The restaurant's clientele craned their necks between bites to see what all the commotion was about.

"Oh, and keep the change, young man. You deserve it," Garrison said. He held out his hand to Tessie, who was dabbing perspiration from her forehead with a cloth napkin.

"But, Garrison," she croaked. Although she longed with every fiber of her being to rip that obscenely large tip from the waiter's grasp, Tessie was grimly aware of the decorum demanded by this awkward situation. Limply, she took Garrison's hand and walked slowly by his side out of the restaurant.

05
The Ice Age Cometh

Tessie glared at Garrison as they drove home from the restaurant. She hated the way her husband gripped the steering wheel with both hands. He sat ramrod straight in an oddly formal position, as if bracing against a bout of gastrointestinal distress he hoped no one else would notice. He refused to take his eyes off the road for even a second to look at her. Tessie thought she hadn't been that tense driving a vehicle since the fateful night over 40 years ago when she'd "borrowed" the keys to her daddy's car and swerved up to lovers' peak to relinquish her virginity to Buzz Chew, Valhalla High School's star quarterback.

I can't believe I married such a candy-ass geek, she thought, relieved to ease her mind with some good old-fashioned bitchiness. It helped take the edge off her mounting fury at the way the evening had turned out. Tessie struggled to contain her anger. Her plan was to torture Garrison with stony silence during their drive home and throughout the remainder of the weekend if necessary, since she knew on some primal level that he took refuge in the exchange of words, no matter how unpleasant. *This sucks,* Tessie thought. *He's too busy with his pathetic driving to notice that I'm freezing him out. Fuck it—I'm gonna let him have it!*

Tessie leaned close to her husband, who was

53

staring myopically through the windshield, now splattered with raindrops. Impassively, he flicked on the windshield wipers. The blades began rhythmically slapping an arc across the plexiglass.

"Have you lost your fucking mind?" Tessie shrieked her contempt directly into Garrison's ear. He gave a spasmodic start, levitating from his seat.

"Jesus Chriiiiiiist!" he shouted and wrenched the steering wheel hard to the right. The car lurched abruptly to the side of the road, tires squealing. "You could have killed us both, you lunatic," he screamed.

Garrison and Tessie sat catching their breath, glaring at each other across the divide of the bucket seats. The wipers continued to move with an insistent cadence across the windshield, casting eerie, flickering shadows across their faces. As she sat in the dark, Tessie was surprised to feel her body tingle with happiness and relief. Finally, she had gotten Garrison's full attention. She with the crude conversational skills and lack of sophistication he always found so embarrassing. Triumphantly, Tessie seized the opportunity to get her point across.

"You prance around like you're some fuckin' prince," she hissed. "You think you're smarter than everyone else—Mr. Mensa; Mr. 'I've got a soiree to attend.' Well, I've got news for you, you sorry prick—

you're no better than me. And where do you get off blowing that kind of cash on a total stranger when you won't even spring for cable TV? And look at these rags I'm wearing—when was the last time you gave me money for some decent clothes?"

"I'm not listening to this," Garrison snarled, flooring the gas pedal. The car veered back onto the highway with an ear-rending screech. Tessie's head snapped back hard at the sudden acceleration, but she kept yelling. The torrent of bile she'd unleashed had taken on a life of its own. She would not—could not —stop venting.

"Don't you shut me out!" she screamed. "Who the Hell do you think you are? I will not be made to feel like a worthless piece of shit ever again, do you hear me?"

"Too late," Garrison said under his breath.

"Oh, fuck you. So that's how it's going to be?" Tessie's shrieks had diminished to a menacing whisper, which Garrison found infinitely more unsettling. He was used to dealing with his loud, abrasive wife, not this savagely muted creature. *Now I've really done it*, Garrison thought, instantly regretting his last remark. He glanced furtively over at Tessie, who was now subdued, but still clearly seething as she glared at him, choking back sobs and roughly wiping tears from her cheek.

Now she's too quiet, Garrison thought with a rush of apprehension. *This can't be good.*

Garrison's mood spiraled into a pit of darkness as he gunned the accelerator, knowing full well that getting home a few minutes faster could only deepen his problems. Still, he felt some comfort in catapulting the car into the gloom. The dreary night seemed such a cozy metaphor for his deteriorating state of mind.

They drove on, wipers swaying like twin metronomes, lulling Garrison and Tessie into a sustained, hostile silence. During the rest of the ride home, they sat as far apart as the confines of the car would allow. Garrison tried to clear away his troubled thoughts by focusing on the road, which kept rushing up breathlessly to flow beneath his speeding vehicle, like a relentlessly advancing tide.

06
A Man of Wealth and Taste

Garrison sat on the examining table, waiting for the doctor to come in. Stripped of his perennial polo shirt and crisp khakis, he felt like an imposter about to be caught with his pants down—literally. Shivering, he clutched at his flimsy patient's gown, trying to gather it around his pale flesh, which at the moment was clad only in boxer shorts. Garrison flipped impatiently through *Money Magazine*, but couldn't drum up his usual enthusiasm for the articles inside, shrilly trumpeting the latest financial bromides.

At the rate I'm going, I won't be around to stress-test my retirement fund, he thought. Tossing the magazine aside, he gave himself over to the naked act of simply waiting. He sat there and fidgeted in the cold, clinical room, in which not one aesthetically redeeming decoration was displayed to distract him. Instead, his eyes were drawn to a lone, garish painting of a red crab straddling some shards of blue pottery. The crab looked disenfranchised, as if out of place in its own exoskeleton. Garrison found himself rooting for the hapless crustacean, wishing it could escape the cruel imprisonment of exaggerated brush strokes and scuttle to some watery oasis.

Clearly, a Paint By Numbers abomination, he thought disdainfully. But even this sneering critique of the doctor's decorator failed to cheer Garrison up.

I'm not sure what's worse, Garrison thought. *Being trapped alone in a tiny, airless room with this ghastly painting or knowing that the doctor will arrive soon to confirm that my brain's out of commission.*

As much as Garrison longed for good news, he knew he wouldn't be getting any. Since that disturbing incident in the corporate training room several months ago when his mind had gone blank, and he couldn't answer Rudy's simple networking question, things had gone from bad to worse. It was as if his brain would simply decide to stop cooperating without a moment's notice. He'd stride purposefully into a room to get something and end up standing there at a complete loss—without the foggiest notion of why he'd entered. He was even having trouble balancing his checkbook; his chicken scratch entries, which had always been illegibly accurate before, now insisted on adding up differently each time he attempted to reconcile the figures. That very week, mortified at being bested by such a trifling task (*a man of his mathematical heft*), he'd flown into a rage, breaking a window in his study and flushing his checkbook and calculator unceremoniously down the toilet.

Alarmed by the racket, Tessie had rushed into the room. There she'd stood, as if nailed to the floor, gawking at his outburst. Then she did something that seemed odd to Garrison upon mulling (and wincing) over this painful incident a few days later. She'd pulled out her flip phone and taken a picture of him, manic and distraught leaning against the bathroom wall, his chest heaving as he stared at the rivulets of blood flowing down his lacerated hands.

"Good Morning! Sorry to keep you waiting." Garrison hadn't heard the knock at the door and looked up startled. His field of vision was suddenly crowded by a tall, imposing figure in blindingly white scrubs. This had to be Dr. Stone, the eminent neurologist. He was so tan, he looked burnished. Garrison squinted up at this bronzed testament to testosterone and stuck out his hand. The doctor grasped his palm collegially in an warmly authoritative and deeply cushioned handshake.

Only CEOs and priests have handshakes like that, thought Garrison. *Powerful pontificators*. Garrison chuckled to himself, pleased by the impromptu alliteration.

Doctor Stone sat down on a stool opposite the examining table and peered intently into Garrison's face. Garrison couldn't help but sheepishly admire the doctor's patrician posture, since the best he could manage at the moment was a dejected slump, which at least kept his skimpy gown from gaping too lewdly.

"Mr. Hand, I've had the opportunity to review

your CAT Scan, and I'd like to discuss the various outcomes the test results present. You see, your prognosis is by no means set in stone. How you choose to care for your health over the coming months can have a significant impact."

Garrison was seized with an overwhelming desire to burst out laughing. *What's this pompous ass gonna do when he examines me and gets a load of the "Fruitcake is Evil" logo on my skivvies,* he thought with irrepressible glee, which he knew was totally inappropriate, given the circumstances. He still smiled every time he pulled on that ridiculous underwear, a gag gift one Christmas from his young, data center trainees.

"Mr. Hand, are you with me?" Dr. Stone asked, his friendly tone now weighted with gravitas.

"What? Ah ... yes I am, Doc," Garrison replied with forced enthusiasm, trying to drag himself back into the solemnity of the moment. "Whatever's left of me. Sorry I drifted off just then. That's been happening to me a lot lately. So—don't sugar-coat it. It's Alzheimer's, right?"

Dr. Stone shifted his weight lithely on the stool. "I'm not convinced that labeling your condition would prove productive at the moment," he said.

"Suffice it to say that you're suffering from a deterioration in cognitive function that certainly could fall within the Alzheimer's spectrum. The thing is—I'm aware of your history of alcoholism. How we're able to manage the challenge of controlling your behavior going forward could have a substantial effect on your overall well-being."

Garrison hung his head, feeling chastened by the doctor's formal tone—not to mention impeccable diction. "I *have* had a little relapse, Doc," he said balefully. "But nothing too drastic. It's the wife. You know how it is—or then again maybe you don't—but she drives me to drink, literally!"

"Mr. Hand," Dr. Stone interjected with the solemn, measured cadence of a clergyman administering Last Rites. "Please allow me to be candid. Your wife will be the least of your problems if you persist in taking even one more drink. Alcohol consumption is no longer an option for you. Amyloid disease is already attacking the blood vessels in your brain, which are becoming increasingly brittle and frail. Keep drinking, and you'll surely succumb to a stroke. You've already suffered some minor bleeds to the brain that are the likely cause of the onset dementia symptoms you've described in your patient history."

Dr. Stone paused, still maintaining eye contact with Garrison, who found the doctor's laser beam intensity perversely humbling. After all, he had always been the one to be reckoned with in academic and professional circles, where he enjoyed some notoriety as the scintillating scoundrel, the Wit at large. Now, however, he'd been reduced to enduring a lecture from this self-satisfied imposter *(yes—that's what he clearly was),* who didn't hesitate to talk down to him as if he were some snot-nosed schoolboy.

Summoning the remnants of his dignity, Garrison slid off the examining table onto his feet. He stood as tall as possible, straining to elongate his spine, but was still obliged to peer up into the doctor's chiseled (and well-exfoliated) face.

"Dr. Stone, I'll have you know that you're not the only distinguished guy in this room. I am a proud Amherst alum and—what else? Oh, yes, a Fulbright Scholar. In my spare time, when I wasn't jet-setting to promote global enlightenment, I managed to build a nifty little technology start-up that went on to inflict shock and awe on the IPO market! I could go on, but my schedule is double-booked as usual, and I really must get back to the office." Pleased with the crispness of his exposition, Garrison fixed his most withering gaze on Dr. Stone, hoping to make him squirm. Unfortunately, after what seemed like a small eternity, a rogue particle wafted into Garrison's eye, which started to blink and twitch spasmodically.

Sensing that his window for wowing the good doctor with his personal pedigree was closing, Garrison grabbed his clothes off the hook on the back of the examining room door and swept out into the hermetically-sealed hospital corridor, almost colliding with a nurse who was crossing its gleaming expanse.

She looked at Garrison quizzically. "Are – you – OK – Sir?" she asked very loudly, punctuating each word with a pregnant pause as if addressing a mental patient.

Before Garrison could respond, Dr. Stone dashed out of the examining room. "Mr. Hand, where do you think you're going?" he asked, looking uncharacteristically perturbed.

Garrison, pretending not to hear words uttered by persons in white coats, stuck his nose in the air and strode away. He couldn't resist peeking back, however, noticing with some satisfaction that Dr. Stone and the nurse looked properly disconcerted and seemed to be engaged in anxious discussion. Elated that he'd thrown the medical establishment off-kilter, Garrison continued to triumphantly exit the building, although the well-buffed floors nearly caused him to slip several times.

This building is a death trap, he thought smugly. He soldiered on to the parking lot, where his car was conveniently parked just where he'd left it. A big relief, since he couldn't seem to find his car anymore without first pressing his key fob's panic button. He reached into his pocket automatically for his keys, but his hand kept sliding unencumbered down his leg. Garrison groaned in disbelief. Somehow, in all the excitement, he'd forgotten to put on his street clothes; he was still dressed in that horrible hospital gown! Even worse, where were his keys? There was no way in hell he'd even consider going back inside that institution of iniquity now to retrieve them.

"Looking for these?" It was the nurse, who'd followed him outside. She was holding something out to him in her manly, chapped hands.

Just like a longshoreman's, he thought. Then he realized that she'd brought him his shoes, which he must have left in the examining room. Irritated at his own idiocy, he grabbed for them roughly, knocking a shoe out of the nurse's grasp. Something else fell to the pavement, as well, with a clatter. He bent over to get a better look, and there glinting on the ground were his keys.

What jackass stuck these in my shoe? he thought.

⊰ 07 ⊱
Tessie Unplugged

Winter, 2003

Tessie stepped out of the shower and wrapped her wet, flowing hair in a plush towel. Thick steam filled the bathroom, and she smeared the fog off the mirror, leaning over the pedestal sink to take a closer look at her face. A pale oval shrouded in mist peered back. Annoyed, Tessie grabbed a tissue and assailed the mirror with several vigorous strokes.

"There, that's better," she said as her image came into focus. Tessie preened, turning her head from side to side to study her face from various angles. She contorted her mouth and raised her eyebrows to accentuate the hollow of her checks and smooth the laugh lines framing her glimmering dark eyes.

Tessie had long since recognized the inconvenient reality that she was no longer young. Recognition did not mean surrender in her book, however. She navigated her 50s with rugged resourcefulness. For Tessie, chasing the trappings of prolonged youth was no more daunting than bagging a tiger might be for a big game hunter on safari. Of course, the closest she'd ever come to scoring a kill was ordering the jumbo freezer pack at the local butcher's. Wrestling 20 pounds of prime fillet and chicken cutlet into the trunk of her car was no mean feat (especially when it was already overflowing with her latest fashion acquisitions: satin bomber jacket, crystal-encrusted jeans, fur-trimmed cardigan, Vuitton Rainbow Bag).

Tessie did not believe in embracing those feminine flaws that become exaggerated with advancing age. Nor did she find the remotest solace in accentuating her inner beauty. She wasn't even sure what this new age phenomenon meant when she'd first read about it in *Marie Claire*.

How can something you can't see be beautiful? she'd thought dismissively. By the time she was pregnant with her youngest child, Buddy, she was certain that the character-building sacrifices of motherhood could not even begin to compensate for her stretch-marked belly and slightly sagging breasts.

"OH – MY – GOD," she'd shrieked while examining her body under the fluorescent spotlights of the Magnificent Maternity dressing room. "Since when did my tits start dangling like string cheese!"

This watershed moment launched Tessie's ongoing trek through the perilous wasteland of physical perfectionism, where emaciated supplicants chase an eternally fleeting, air-brushed idol. That is, when they're not busy genuflecting at the feet of some winking shaman, aka plastic surgeon.

Though never one to analyze the past, Tessie would on occasion think back on simpler times, before she needed a fierce mastery of feminine artifice.

While drenching her tension away in a hot shower, she'd often let her mind wander through such memories, an indulgence she found soothing after an irritating day.

Tessie was a scion of first-generation Italian parents, who clung doggedly to an old world view that helped buffer them from the stark realities of life in Newark, NJ, which was poised on the brink of industrial decline and divisive urban renewal when she was a teenager in the early 60s. Every Saturday night, her brothers would spend hours dressing up to go out like professional sartorialists—snapping trouser straps into position, buffing cufflinks to a high gloss, applying pomade to patent-slick hair. Their raucous laughter and horseplay would reverberate throughout their parents' little cape house. Once they were polished and prepped for an evening of gambling, wine, women and song (not necessarily in that order), the boys would spill out onto tree-lined Linden Avenue, and Tessie could hear them joking all the way to Conway Street, roughhousing as they ran.

She would stay at home in her cotton shift. Her parents, who worked ceaselessly to keep the family plastering business going, relied on her to keep house and cook. She did so without question; the race riots that came later that decade had yet to explode social conventions. She'd dutifully make the Braciole and gravy, and then serve it to her parents on TV trays. Every night religiously, they'd plant themselves in front of their Zenith's flickering, black and white screen to watch *The Price Is Right*. Relieved to have temporarily stilled their chronic bickering (complete with operatic flailing for emphasis), she'd actually look forward to the main event of her evening— washing the Venetian blinds.

Hunched over the claw foot bathtub (which she didn't know was vintage at the time), Tessie would lose herself in the pleasantly numbing repetition of this chore, submerging the barely soiled blinds in a warm, sudsy solution of ammonia and Palmolive— dipping and swirling, scrubbing and dunking. Her mother had been scandalized that Tessie insisted on performing this traditional task on Saturday evenings, when everyone knows that self-respecting girls scour the blinds first thing Saturday morning. Adjusting the schedule of her domestic drudgery was Tessie's first act of defiance.

It would soon dawn on her, however, that there was a bigger world out there than could be contained within the disinfected parameters of her parent's tiny home. One day, while patching the frayed damask wallpaper that lent a moth-eaten formality to the vestibule, Tessie began to wonder why she was salvaging the very walls that were closing in around her.

She had also started to notice alarming changes in her own body, which were causing her to question everything in her routine-bound life that she'd previously accepted at face value. Her once scrawny, school-girlish figure was now refusing to conform to her parents' strict code of propriety. (Those strictures of chaste obedience that they'd drum into her "pretty" head, yet summarily toss aside when it came to her wild and worldly brothers. (*After all, boys will be boys.*))

Tessie would sneak away to her room just to take a private peak at her new, insubordinate body. What she saw framed in the patinaed gilt of her bedroom mirror made her feel both exhilarated and deeply apologetic—like she'd better make a beeline for the confessional booth (conveniently ensconced in the Immaculate Conception church just three blocks over).

Her new breasts, alone, cried out for atonement. Previously meager at best, they'd now burgeoned to buoyantly lush proportions. *Just like that picture of Bombay Mangos in National Geographic,* she'd thought.

Her hips, too, had taken on a mind of their own. Bony before, they now curved aggressively—echoing the hard, feminine sweep of the violins pictured on the jacket of that Bing Crosby LP her mother played over and over on their stackable turntable.

Her breasts and hips weren't all that had changed. Tessie could no longer stroll anonymously to the corner market. Now she attracted attention.

The neighborhood lawn boy was the first one to notice her new image. As she passed by, he leaned back from his exertions at the push reel mower, stretching and yawning extravagantly. (Tessie wondered when he'd become prone to sudden-onset fatigue.)

The lawn boy pulled the kerchief from around his thick, blotchy neck and mopped his forehead, staring at her from beneath his low-slung, sweaty brow. His lips pulled back in a rictus of lust, exposing both rows of nubby, stained teeth. Tessie was startled. The only point of reference she had for such an alarming grimace was yet another National Geographic article she'd glanced through, detailing the arboreal mating habits of Indonesian Orangutans.

After this eye-opening encounter, Tessie learned to more gracefully deflect the heated advances of the local boys. At first, their clammy attentions made her feel violated, as if she were complicit in some venal act. She fretted that her new status as an object of desire had somehow shamed her family, which could only result in her staunchly Catholic parents casting her out on the street. Before long, however, Tessie looked forward to such an ejection and the unprecedented freedom it would bring. She realized that her carnal appeal was her only way out and began working her bombshell bonafides with confidence. By the time she met Frank (fated to become husband number one), she was primed to press the first viable man she met into service and marry her way out of Newark.

And so, Frank's fate was sealed. Blithely unaware of the advancing juggernaut of his future wife's ambition, he was working a new construction job with Tessie's father down on Conway, when she stopped by with sandwiches and beer for the workmen. Frank was precariously balanced on a step ladder spackling seams in the sheetrock when he heard footsteps coming up behind him. He turned and promptly dropped his trowel at the sight of Tessie's siron silhouette, splattering them both with gobs of plaster. Tessie let loose an impatient little shriek and stomped her foot. Hands on hips, she fixed Frank with a blistering stare as he scrambled down the ladder.

"Good Heavens, Miss. I'm – I'm awfully sorry," he stammered, reaching out to wipe the plaster from her blouse and then (on second thought) sheepishly pulling back his hand.

Tessie smoothed her skirt with an imperious flick of the wrist and then (without missing a beat) rearranged her pout into a dazzling smile.

"I suppose you'll have to make it up to me," she said, her voice oozing with honey. "Of course, the dry cleaning bill will be a fortune, and I'm not even sure they can get these horrid stains out."

"This – this – this is terrible," Frank stuttered, his mind churning with competing visions of Tessie's plaster-flecked bosom and the discomforting prospect of his boss's fury upon seeing the ruined dress.

"I'll take care of the cleaning bill, Miss," Frank said, dizzy from gazing into the dark vortex of Tessie's eyes. *Her lashes are thicker than Bambi's,* he thought, barely able to suppress the hysterical confession of love straining to burst from his lips.

"I'll make sure your father knows I'm making this right," Frank gushed, helplessly sensing that he had turned down a dangerous path. Indeed, he did consult Tessie's father, who far from being angry, seized on the opportunity to pawn his daughter off on a decent guy before she became too wild to control. (Sure, Frank was a bit, well, *slow* and hopelessly naïve—but Tessie's dad figured she'd be just the girl to accelerate the young man's maturation.)

Not long after, Tessie managed to nimbly parlay

several awkward dinner dates with Frank into a far more enduring date with destiny at the altar.

At the jarring thought of her first wedding day, Tessie shook her head vigorously to dislodge the sepia visual of Frank's adoring gaze, which even now seemed to swallow her up. The towel she'd coiled around her damp hair came loose and, leaning over to give it a twist, she struck her head on the bathroom sink, literally jolting herself back to reality.

No more playing wifey to love sick Frank in that little house with the white picket fence, she thought. *This is the new millennium, and you're married to Garrison now—a bigger diva than you are.* She chuckled at the thought of Garrison's most recent bout of hypochondria, which had sent him scurrying to yet another specialist—some kind of brain doctor this time.

A series of electronic trills rang out from the master bedroom. She pulled her robe around her, sprinted to the bedside table, and grabbed the phone.

"Hullo there" rasped the voice on the other end of the line. "How's my gorgeous mamasita?"

"Baby Boy," she cooed. "It's late—is everything ok?"

"I threw my back out again, Ma, but it's nothing a few Jack and Cokes can't fix. How *you* doing?"

"Well, your stepdad's driving me nuts—male menopause or something—but whaddya gonna do?" Tessie said with a playful shrug, plopping down on the bed. She always looked forward to talking with Buddy, her youngest (and favorite) child, but fervently hoped his chronic complaining wouldn't intensify the migraine that was building after her collision with the bathroom sink.

"Go easy on the poor bastard," Buddy teased. "He's put up with your crazy shit for what—50 years now?"

"28—watch it," Tessie shot back with a chuckle.

Buddy and his mother shared a rapport that had miraculously weathered her nasty divorce from his father, Frank. Almost 30 years later, this painfully drawn-out conflict still stirred up Buddy's rawest emotions. Back when he was a kid, the neighbors used to whisper that the dissolution of Tessie and Frank's union had taken longer than any other divorce in the history of the county. Buddy could still recall the feral zeal with which Tessie had fought for every stick of furniture. Even the family's ancient, banged up toboggan had been hotly contested during the division of assets. Tessie did manage to end up with the toboggan, but somehow Buddy and his sisters weren't as neatly accounted for.

Although Tessie had been obsessed with separating Frank from his living room coffee table, along with each and every warped coaster he'd ever set a can of beer on, she wasn't nearly as enthusiastic about appropriating her own children. Buddy had other ideas, though. He couldn't afford to let Tessie vanish from his life. A hypersensitive, brooding kid, he was deeply invested in preserving his role as "baby of the family" and wasn't about to let some stupid old divorce wreck his special status. Over the years, his tenacity had paid off, and Tessie warmed to the flattery of his enduring attentions. Campaigning for his mother's loyalty was the only project that Buddy had ever stuck with. As Tessie bailed him out financially time and time again with dogged determination, Buddy was empowered to follow the path of least resistance: routinely discarding college classes, girlfriends, jobs, social obligations, even personal hygiene—whatever smacked of consistency or conformity. He did manage to sustain one commitment, however—a deep and personal relationship with an impressive array of illicit drugs.

"Well, Garrison's not the only guy with problems, Ma. I've got a few of my own right now," Buddy said.

"What's the matter now? It's not that little whore you're living with, is it? That tattoo model with the

79

piercings?"

"No, Ma. She's been gone for weeks now. Her tattoos clashed so bad I couldn't even look at her without getting cross-eyed. Wait a minute, why are we even talking about this? I actually really need a new car. My Honda had a little, ah, mishap—on the Belt Parkway. But don't worry, I'm OK."

"Oh My God, Buddy. What happened? Were you smoking that Chronic-ass weed she keeps lying around? That little low life—I knew she'd finally fuck you over one of these days. I told you to lay off the strong shit. Damn, I should have made you go to college. I can't believe I bought your bullshit about the world coming to an end, and how you wouldn't have time to graduate anyway. Well, if the apocalypse is coming, it's 20 fucking years too late. My bank account's dying a slow death, though, as it funnels directly into your pocket. Jeez!"

Tessie stopped ranting just long enough to catch her breath. She heaved a deep sigh of resignation. "Ok, Buddy. How much do you need this time?"

Tessie dropped the phone into its cradle, falling back onto her bed with a dull thud. *Could this headache get any worse?* she wondered, clutching her temples and closing her eyes. Despite taking self-congratulatory solace in Buddy's frequent phone calls —she must have done *something* right raising him— she now felt totally depleted, as she did each time Buddy ambushed her with one of his sob stories.

Tessie drifted off into an uneasy miasma of dreams. In her out-of-body state, she felt herself plummet down a steep shaft, hitting bottom with a resounding (yet strangely unimpactful) thud. Chaffing against the stifling enclosure, Tessie tried to break free by frantically flailing and rocking. It dawned on her that her body had now become as ethereal as breath fogging glass. Tessie relaxed into this new-found lack of anatomy and allowed herself to waft into the next dreamscape. She soared effort-lessly above a bright, verdant meadow, unruly with wildflowers and fragrant honeysuckle, festooned at its outer reaches with lush, blackberry brambles. *Just like Nona's old pasture,* she thought.

But wait—gliding down through a dazzle of sunbeams into dappled shadows beneath a stand of stately elms, Tessie glimpsed something moving— she didn't know what. She drifted closer.

Nestled among the blackberry bushes was a hirsute man-child, ungainly limbs twitching and lacerating against the thorny briar, as he ravenously suckled a debauchery of ripe, abundant breast. *But who, who is that girl?* Tessie tilted aloft on an ethereal breeze to circle around this strange tableau. The face of the woman attached to the gluttonous teat came slowly into view. With a flash of recognition and horror, Tessie dove into a screaming spiral, directly into the yawning maw of her worst nightmare.

Tessie awakened with a start and sat bolt upright in bed, sweat and tears streaming down her face. Normally, she wasn't stirred by nuance of any kind, let alone dream interpretations, but the visceral impact of this vision was a punch to the gut.

"Shit," she gasped, nearly choking on her own saliva. "That was *my* boob, and the big, furry fuckwit latched onto it was Buddy."

"Christ, I've got to get my hands on the rest of Garrison's money," she shrieked at no one in particular, succumbing to a full-on tantrum.

"If I can't figure this out—find a way to convince Garrison—Buddy will suck me dry, and I won't be able to help him anymore." Tessie continued to project her voice across the large bedroom, challenging her encroaching desperation.

Swayed by vertigo, Tessie gripped the bed. "Fuckin' A! He'll never agree to fork over his investments, not the shit-load Buddy needs, anyway," she cried.

Tessie sank back into bed, clutching her throbbing head. "Garrison will just lecture me on tough love, and how it's the only way to make Buddy change his self-destructive habits. But he doesn't know Buddy like I do. My son is too sensitive for this shitshow of a world. He'll be eaten alive if I don't do something—fast," she whispered hoarsely behind her tears.

Unaccustomed to the novelty of such strenuous thought, Tessie curled up into the fetal position, too overwhelmed to notice Garrison standing just outside their bedroom door.

08
Love and Loathing

It was time for drastic measures. This much was obvious to Garrison as he stood in a state of paralysis, taking in Tessie's bizarre bedroom outburst.

She never could keep her trap shut, but this is ridiculous! Stunned by the revelations Tessie had spewed, Garrison struggled to make sense of it all.

Thank God she doesn't know I'm listening out here, or she'd really go berserk. Garrison hunched over, sickened by her betrayal. How that poor schlub Buddy ever got a word in edgewise with his mother was completely beyond him—not that he gave a rat's ass about the perverse details of their relationship.

But how to stop Tessie? Garrison knew she was smarter than she looked. He had to do something definitive—and fast—to protect his daughters' financial future before his mind gave out entirely, and Tessie absconded with everything!

But Garrison wasn't feeling especially clever lately. In fact, he wondered if he could ever rekindle his former brilliance—that sputtering lightening in a bottle.

So much for my so-called towering intellect, thought Garrison. *Damn that doctor! I wish he'd just break down and give me a straightforward diagnosis. I refuse to lose my mind to some vague, boutique affliction.*

Garrison's predicament was slowing coming

into focus. If he flew off the handle and divorced Tessie, she'd tie up his assets for years. Or if he tried to sneak some iron-clad legalese into his will, she'd be on to him and throw herself into making his life a living hell.

Christ, I can't even remember my lawyer's name at the moment. Maybe it'll come back to me tomorrow. Garrison strained to think, but his beleaguered mind failed to produce a coherent plan. *But I can't wait until tomorrow. I've gotta do something today, before I totally lose my grip,* he despaired.

Garrison tried to corral his frantic thoughts— an exercise in futility. A wave of emotional exhaustion and low blood sugar suddenly engulfed him. Feeling faint, he limped downstairs to the kitchen and collapsed on a stool at the center island. He was famished by this time, but didn't know what he wanted to eat. Glancing around the kitchen for inspiration, his eyes darted across the tumbled glass backsplash, gleaming granite countertops and custom-glazed cabinetry, which Tess had insisted on.

Sweet Mother of God. That's it! Garrison leapt to his feet, swept up in a hallelujah moment. The answer to his Tessie problem was right there—conveniently stacked in the pantry and staring him in the face.

Garrison eased open the door to Tess's bathroom as gingerly as possible. He was pretty sure she'd gone out shopping, but was still paranoid he'd get caught red-handed in her private sanctuary.

OK, he exhaled. *First hurdle cleared.* Garrison crept across the tile floor to the medicine cabinet. He stood there for what seemed an eternity, feeling like a heretic about to deface a sacred shrine. Finally, he inhaled sharply and pulled open the cabinet door, revealing a gleaming array of cosmetic jars, lined up neatly like high-end soldiers.

She really does have the instincts of a drill sergeant, Garrison thought, as he envisioned Tessie vigorously slathering on lotions each night to smother insidious signs of aging. His initial anxiety was giving way to a creeping numbness, but he was keenly aware there could be no turning back.

Garrison glanced over the gilded phalanx of labels again. It was like deciphering a foreign language: Retinol Rescue, Skintillation Serum, Derm Epiphany.

How could she possibly apply all these concoctions on a daily basis, he wondered? It didn't matter. He had to open at least one glossy jar—with extreme caution. He knew Tess would immediately pick up on clumsy tampering.

Fuck this shit. I'll go for the epiphany stuff. Garrison grabbed the jar and wrenched off the cap. He fished a small tin from his back pocket and pulled back the metal ring, exposing closely-packed escargots, which he'd retrieved from the kitchen earlier. With shaking hands, he poured a few drops of the pungent snail oil into the cosmetics jar, stirred the emulsion with a Q-Tip and carefully placed the jar back in the cabinet.

Mission accomplished. Garrison hummed a Chopin dirge as he turned on his heel and fled the room.

⤳ 09 ⤶
Buyer's Remorse

Garrison awoke with a start as the first rays of sunlight breached his bedroom window. Groaning, he rolled over in bed to block the encroaching light.

"What an ungodly hour," he moaned, rubbing his weary eyes. From sheer force of habit, Garrison cast a listless glance over at Tessie, who lay sleeping by his side.

Damn! You don't look half bad, old girl—especially when you're so enticingly mute. Garrison was caught off guard by his enthused reaction to Tessie's all-too-familiar face. His estranged wife's supine, aquiline loveliness had felled him once again, like a smitten schoolboy. Garrison knew he had to snap out of it, but couldn't quite pinpoint why. He had this nagging feeling that indulging his tender impulses on this morning—of all mornings—would be wildly inappropriate. *What the hell's wrong with me?* Garrison smacked his head reflexively, a bit more energetically than intended.

Still, it really is amazing how—what's the word? —taut you look this morning, Tess, he marveled. Given his busy work schedule, there was rarely time to admire his wife by the sepia light of dawn, no matter how amorous his mood. He was dumbstruck by the dramatic freshness of her smooth, rosy face. The unbidden image of a tightly encased Andouille sausage sprang to mind.

91

Shaking his head to dislodge this last, disturbing visual, Garrison carefully rolled out of bed to avoid waking Tessie and crept into the shower. He lost track of time performing his ablutions, trying to clear his head with brisk slaps of Savage Essentials aftershave. When he finally emerged from the bathroom, 30 minutes had sped by.

Tessie was still lying in bed just as he'd left her, but now the room was brighter, and she looked different somehow. Garrison walked over and laid his hand gingerly on his wife's shoulder. Tessie was unresponsive; her body felt unnaturally stiff. In a panic, Garrison grabbed his glasses from the bedside table to take a closer look. It was now plain to see that the flushed firmness of her skin, which he'd admired in the semi-darkness of early morning, was actually inflamed flesh, engorged to an angry, mottled purple. "Oh Sweet Jesus, what have I done?" Garrison cried out as he began to remember with sickening clarity.

The backstory came to him first. It seemed like yesterday when he and Tessie had celebrated their 20th wedding anniversary at Central Park's Tavern on the Green. Garrison ordered the Honey Roasted Fig appetizer, while Tessie chose the escargot. Unfortunately, their bucolic dinner ended badly. Halfway through slurping down a few butter-slick snails, Tessie began clutching her neck, wheezing and writhing violently. After an initial commotion, as a crush of concerned patrons gathered around this spectacle, the maître d' summoned an ambulance, which whisked Tessie to New York Presbyterian's emergency room.

As distant memories of this celebratory, turned-anaphylactic evening came flooding back, Garrison realized it would take more than the mere prick of an EpiPen to undo his transgressions of the previous evening.

Did I really manage to poison her? Garrison winced as he finally recalled sneaking into Tessie's bathroom to spike her face cream with the same slimy delicacy that had almost killed her at dinner years before.

Desperate for air, Garrison dropped his bathrobe, grabbed his pants and t-shirt off the bedroom floor, and dashed out the front door.

10

An Uncommon Fete

As he stumbled away from the house, Garrison braced himself against the winter chill. The lightweight t-shirt he'd just pulled on couldn't insulate his shivering flesh from the glacial air outside.

Mountaineers get frostbite scaling the heights, not geriatrics like me strolling at street-level. Garrison paused for a moment to rub his rapidly numbing hands together. *I'll be OK — I just bought that obscenely expensive blizzard fleece.*

Garrison sniffed to reassure himself and continued slogging down the snowy sidewalk. The notion that he'd better head back to retrieve his new warm coat from the closet—along with any flannel shirt within reach—never crossed his mind. After all, admitting to an error in judgment would be at odds with the lofty, Ivy League veneer he worked so hard to cultivate.

Garrison's neighborhood was woodsy and bucolic, in a self-consciously suburban way. He soon trudged by a farm stand boarded up for the winter. The last time he'd noticed this rustic, plywood structure was during the previous summer, while riding by on his bike. His spirits had lifted to see the seasonal reemergence of this quaint, roadside cornucopia, overflowing with unblemished, photo-ready produce—a harbinger of July's beachfront delights.

Ever an embarrassment of riches out here on the East End, Garrison mused. *Imperfections are not to be tolerated!*

Garrison continued walking past the tall hedgerows and venerable elms bordering the lush acreage that surrounded his neighbors' carriage houses and summer cottages (discreet code names for mansions). Just beyond these landscaped estates, Jungle Pete's bar came into view, a favorite haunt of the local havenots. During the formative years of his marriage, Garrison had whiled away many an evening at this rustic establishment. It was easier to drink himself senseless than grapple with the unsavory reality that his marriage was a disaster.

Garrison had taken sheepish pleasure in mingling with the bar's local denizens, most of whom eked out a modest living working the land or sea. At night, the shingled bungalow's windows lit up like aquarium glass for the benefit of passersby, who could clearly observe the unruly press of townsfolk elbowing their way up to the bar. Fishermen, gardeners, town dump laborers, struggling artists and writers, alike, crowded in to quench a communal thirst.

Garrison stood staring nostalgically at the place; he'd never had to prove anything there. The humanity gathered within those walls had endured bone-deep disappointment, chronic unemployment or backbreaking labor, but no one ever judged—or perhaps he'd been too intoxicated to notice.

And so, the party had always continued into the witching hours, made even more primeval by the lack of street lights. "Dark skies" was a village edict meant to promote immersive star gazing, an amusing novelty for Wall Street's wealthy masters of the universe, who made the East End their summer playground. At closing time, the patrons tumbled out of the bar into the inky, enveloping night, punctuated by stands of scrub pines, an orchestral revelry of crickets, and the luminescent drift of fireflies.

All this strenuous reminiscing made Garrison drowsy. He sat down heavily on a tree stump, conveniently situated on the pub's overgrown front lawn.

It's not appropriate to nap here. Garrison barely had time to process this thought before he slumped over and started to snore.

"C'mon, buddy! Wake up!"
Garrison felt a sturdy grip rock him from side to side.

Hey—fuck off, he thought. But he didn't have time for distractions. He was too busy prepping for his big lecture. It was a minor miracle he'd made it there at all, after nearly freezing to death slogging through snowdrifts to City Hall. Of course, he knew Oslo was nippy during the winter, but he hadn't expected this blast-chiller onslaught! And why the Hell did he forget to pack his new, fleece coat?

For chrissakes, I can't be expected to remember mundane details on this glorious occasion. Garrison peered through a strange haze to get a better look at the imposing murals adorning the great, marble hall. He shuddered with excitement to think he'd actually be accepting a Nobel Peace Prize at a gala there later that evening.

"Hey Gar, it's me, Ricky. Can you hear me? You passed out, Bub. C'mon—lemme get you to your feet. It's too cold to stay out here."

But Garrison was just fine. He was savoring the grand venue, complete with crowds of beautiful Nordic carousers, epic oil paintings and atmospheric echoes. He was trying his best to head over to the banquet they'd laid out in his honor, but this ill-mannered brute kept prodding him. Reluctantly, Garrison allowed his eyes to flutter open, revealing his old friend Ricky Taylor crouched next to him— with Jungle Pete's as an all-too-familiar backdrop.

"You passed out, Buddy. What the fuck were you doing out here anyway? I thought you gave up the hard stuff years ago," Ricky said, his weathered face creased with concern.

Garrison struggled to get his bearings, even as he lingered between an enticing dream-state and encroaching reality, which was far less attractive. The Oslo reverie was *so* seductive, but Garrison felt it slip away as Ricky helped him struggle to his feet.

11
Bitch Redux

Ricky pounded on the front door. His other arm firmly encircled Garrison's waist to keep his friend propped up in a standing position.

How could she let him wander off like this—on the coldest day of the year? The mere thought of Garrison's wife made Ricky grimace with distaste. He'd always thought she was the selfish type that didn't give a rat's ass about anybody but herself. And what's with all that crazy hair and jewelry the size of dinner plates?

No wonder she lost track of Garrison—too busy accessorizing, Ricky thought, his mind drifting for a moment. Garrison started moaning incoherently. Ricky gave him a brawny squeeze.

"There you go, Bub. You'll be warm and toasty in a minute," Ricky said, trying to sound reassuring.

Where is that fuckin' witch? Ricky was seriously annoyed now. He held Tessie fully responsible for the rough shape he'd found his friend in.

I mean it's obvious Garrison's been acting a bit... off...lately. You'd think she'd keep a better eye on him. Ricky was all worked up by this point. He began pounding the door again as hard as he could for what felt like an eternity.

"Tess, Tess," he yelled. "Open up! We got a situation here. Is anybody home?"

Just when Ricky was ready to give up, Tessie

abruptly opened the front door. Startled, he leapt away, nearly falling backwards down the front steps with Garrison in tow. Tessie stood unnaturally still in the doorway, staring blankly into space. Her face was caked with a thick layer of cold cream, like she'd just stepped off the Kabuki stage.

"Uh…uh…uh," Garrison broke into a spasm of tormented grunting, like an animal caught in a steel trap.

"Woah there, buddy." Ricky scrambled to steady Garrison, who had crumpled from shock. A fissure slowly cracked across Tessie's alabaster face. She was smiling.

"This new anti-aging shit is the fuckin' bomb," she croaked, licking her lips indulgently. "I just put more on. My face looks 10 years younger, right?" Ricky could now see that Tessie's mouth was a bulbous vermillion, like the business end of a baboon.

"I finally got the bee sting look I've always wanted," Tessie said stiffly, barely able to move the bloated carnage of her face. She looked down (*probably admiring those Hindenburg lips of hers,* Ricky thought) and suddenly noticed her husband.

"What the Hell's wrong with *him*?" she asked off-handedly.

Ricky didn't bother to answer, pushing Tessie aside as he walked Garrison haltingly into the house.

As the months wore on, Garrison reluctantly came to the realization that he was totally dependent on Tessie's care. Beyond that, he knew only one thing for sure—life would never be the same again.

It had all started the day his friend Ricky drove him home from Jungle Pete's—and there she was. His dead wife standing on their front steps as real as dirt. Granted, Garrison felt his grasp on reality slipping lately. (He preferred to call this encroaching brain fog "cognitive fluidity.") But he still vividly remembered having discovered Tessie's stiff, bloated corpse in their bed that very morning.

Now, not only had Tessie's inert flesh been reanimated, which was disturbing enough, but she turned out to be even more bossy dead than while drawing breath.

Clearly, she lacks the good grace to accept her demise, Garrison reasoned.

During Ricky's weekly visits, Garrison tried to coax him into corroborating their shared, beyond-the-grave sighting, but his friend wouldn't cooperate. In fact, he flatly refused to discuss Tessie's alleged resurrection. Garrison figured that years of potato farming had imposed a literal-minded approach on Ricky, his views as entrenched as the root crops he dug up year after year.

"Just relax, Bub," Ricky would say in an exaggerated "there-there" tone, patting Garrison's shoulder. "You've had a Catty-Wumper of a time. Forget all this crazy shit and just work on getting better. Don't forget—there's no way I'm fishing for snappers at Plover Point without you this summer."

Ricky took a moment to shift uncomfortably in his chair, one of those French country ladder back numbers with a rash-inducing rush seat, which Tessie stationed around the living room to impress (while torturing) her guests.

Ricky leaned in close to Garrison's ear and whispered dramatically, "I tell you what. I wouldn't get inside ten clam rakes of that scary wife of yours if I could help it. Please take care of yourself—and look out for her Up Island lies."

Easier said than done, Garrison thought. *Especially when your dead wife's keeping you sedated in a bathrobe all day. Nurse Ratchet move over!*

Garrison had been too confused to work since his "episode" at Jungle Pete's. At least that's what Tessie called it, when she came into his room one day to administer a skin-abrading sponge bath, and he tried to tell her about the Nobel Peace Prize he'd left back in Oslo.

Brandishing a large loofah and impressive elbow

grease, she leaned in to exfoliate Garrison's back. *This thing is probably teeming with bacteria, but the ergonomic handle gives great torque,* Tessie chuckled to herself. That's when she explained very loudly and slowly that he'd had an episode, and "shit-for-brains" was the only prize he'd be winning today. She managed to talk *at* him—not to him—with a mechanical cadence that was both saccharine and unnerving.

Garrison hadn't liked Tessie much when she still had a pulse, but this dirt-nap reboot of hers was especially annoying. For a supposedly ephemeral spirit, she had quite the knack for being omnipresent and palpably controlling. This eerie state of affairs was getting way too Dickensian for Garrison.

She's like the ghost of Christmas past on crack, Garrison mused. *I mean, aren't the deceased just supposed to fade away? Or if she must linger on, why can't she just stay a disturbing memory?*

Garrison's mind had ample time to wander while he sat strapped into his wheelchair. Although he could still walk fairly well, Tessie sternly admonished that he'd fall and split his head open if he tried to meander around the house. These constant constraints made him all the more eager to escape outside and inspect his garden.

My hybrid tea roses need a good mulching this time of

year. Garrison's special concoction of coffee grounds and eggshells never failed to grow epically lush rose bushes.

Unfortunately, Morticia (his new nickname for Tessie) usually stuck him in the back bedroom, unless people were stopping by. On such occasions, she'd make a big show of wheeling him out to the front porch for some fresh air, putting the "pampered patient" on full display.

NOT, Garrison thought. I mean, I wasn't the perfect husband, but did she have to come back from the bowels of hell to torment me?

He asked Tessie as much during yet another bathtime onslaught. (All this scrubbing and epidermal loss made him feel savaged—and emboldened.)

"Tessie, you've made your point. Please go back to the netherworld where you belong. Rest assured—you've done a perfectly respectable job of torturing me. Your work here is done. The fiery abyss misses you," Garrison said with a gravitas that belied his jangled nerves. Tessie stared at him for a moment and then burst out laughing.

"Oh my God, Mr. Brain Fart here thinks I've come back from the dead. That just confirms his guilty conscience," she muttered to herself with satisfaction. She then focused her withering gaze on

Garrison's shivering, naked body.

"Don't you worry, Sweetheart. When I do decide to head back to the crypt, I'm dragging you down with me. Now hold still while I scrub your filthy armpits."

13
Hoisted with Her Own Petard

Tessie experienced a come-to-Jesus moment (or the atheist equivalent) when she realized Garrison had somehow convinced himself that she'd risen from the dead.

I've never been accused of pulling off a miracle before, let alone one with a religious ring to it. Tessie cringed at the mere thought of her childhood catechism classes. *There's gotta be a way to work this insane situation to Buddy's advantage,* she thought.

Tessie strongly suspected Garrison had something to do with the sudden-onset eczema that had driven her crazy for weeks. First, her lips, eyelids and tongue swelled to elephantine proportions, startling her each time she passed a mirror.

I look like the fuckin' Robert De Niro creature in that Frankenstein movie, she thought peevishly. By the time stinging rashes and blisters had set in, upstaging the swelling, she felt almost relieved. Since Tessie was a strong proponent of "looking good is better than feeling good," she decided to step into the breach once and for all and brave the rigors of tanning bed therapy.

Why can't a girl with oozing sores rock a savage tan? Tessie pouted defensively. Since Garrison had apparently declared war on her world-class complexion, Tessie's mind went into overdrive, hatching schemes to remove him from the picture entirely, while setting Buddy up financially for life. (Granted, her youngest child had always been her favorite, but the goal this time wasn't just to spoil him. Tessie had simply had enough of his endless woe-is-me whining, which had caused her agita ever since she left his father, Frank.)

Tessie thought back to the waning days of her first marriage to Frank, when she'd stuffed an over-sized bag with floral satin bustiers and French-cut, string-tie bikinis for an extended rendezvous with Garrison. *The kids should be happy I'm leaving them behind. How could I possibly raise them on the pathetic alimony Frank can afford to cough up? No, they'll have to get whatever they need directly from their father.*

This illicit assignation with Garrison turned out to be Tessie's de facto disposal of Frank, along with any semblance of their former family life. During the messy divorce proceedings that followed, Tessie had focused her formidable will on seducing Garrison into a marriage proposal—her one-way ticket to the bottom of his deep pockets. Unfortunately, he'd been too drunk or hung-over most of the time to pass erotic muster.

Jeez, a gherkin could outperform this dumb schlub in

the sack, Tessie had scoffed, while watching Garrison sleep off yet another drunken stupor.

Thank God he has other, far more ample assets to keep me amused, Tessie thought with some relief. All she had to do now was keep her eye on the prize and move forward. *Once Garrison and I get married,* she'd told herself, *I'll make it up to the kids.*

Tessie shook her head to dislodge these moldering memories and turned her attention back to the current business at hand. Now that she'd grasped how quickly Garrison was losing his marbles, she had it all figured out. What if she could accelerate his encroaching senility? If she were to "haunt" him, wearing a convincing ghost costume (plus a few dabs of pancake makeup to complete the phantom effect), she could probably drive him over the edge for good. Then there'd be nothing left to stand between her and his lucrative investments.

Tessie bounded upstairs to raid her closet, which was bursting at the seams with glitzy apparel. She unearthed a gauzy, white dress that she'd worn during her fleeting, boho-chic phase, pulling the garment over her head and stepping back to inspect the effect in her full-length mirror. She loved how the gown's translucent tulle seemed to float on air, playing up the raven glory of her lustrous hair.

"And it still fits perfectly," Tessie exclaimed, congratulating herself. (She'd endured many a penitentiary-style diet to stay svelte all these years.) Tessie examined her outfit from every angle. *I need something shimmery to complete the look,* she thought.

Suddenly, a light bulb switched on in Tessie's head. She rushed out to the hall where her extensive jewelry collection was displayed.

A few years back, Tessie had run out of space to exhibit her adornments and nagged Garrison incessantly until he'd reluctantly agreed to rig something up. The hall on the second-floor landing was ideal for repurposing. For one thing, it was the only uncluttered surface left in the house, which she'd crammed with objets d'art.

Halfway through the installation, Garrison had told Tessie he was running out of jewelry organizers to mount on the wall—he needed more hardware to accommodate her "bushels of bling." Tessie remembered he'd run down to the basement and returned with a large fishing tackle box, just as she was heading downstairs to tan in the backyard. She'd laughed

114

at this odd choice of tools and teased him for over-thinking yet another simple task.

"Oh, there's the perfect necklace—way up there," Tessie exclaimed, jumping up and clapping her hands with childlike glee. It was a Victorian cameo, one of her favorite pieces, which she'd hung on the highest hook, above a set of imposing African breastplates.

Tessie positioned an antique, tapestry foot stool beneath the vintage pendant. She stepped gingerly on the wooden frame's domed upholstery, extending her arm as far as she could reach. Tessie's fingertips had just grazed the necklace when the stool's delicate wood frame splintered beneath her feet with a loud, staccato crack.

"Oh crap," Tessie cried out as she lost her balance. She fell face forward, her hands flailing to grab anything that could break her fall. Her body smashed hard against the jewelry-laden wall. As she slid limply to the floor, a razor-sharp display hook sliced cleanly through her jugular. (Garrison must have figured the hook's tempered curved metal, designed to hoist Giant Bluefin Tuna out of the water, would be sturdy enough to hold Tessie's arsenal of hammered-metal, tribal jewelry.)

As Tessie lay twitching and bleeding out on the carpet, her consciousness ignited into a kaleidoscope of Mardi Gras colors. When Garrison's friend Ricky happened to find her a few minutes later, she was curled up in a fetal position, clutching her favorite artisanal necklace—a rough-cut crystal choker.

❦ 14 ❧
The Uninvited Guest

Buddy drove briskly into the West Haven Care lot, jolting and catapulting over several speed bumps before pulling into a parking space. Buddy was nervous about visiting his mother, Tessie, who had just been admitted to the nursing home. He tended to drive erratically when anxiety struck, which happened a lot.

He'd heard about his mom's recent accident from a friend of Garrison's. (Buddy couldn't bring himself to call his mother's current husband—*that philandering prick*—his stepfather.) The friend, Roger or Ricky (*something like that*), had dropped by Tessie's house and found her bleeding on the floor. He'd called an ambulance just in time. Once Tessie had stabilized at the hospital, she'd been quickly transferred to this rehab center. Buddy didn't know any other details, except that his mom was in pretty bad shape.

With a sigh of resignation, Buddy leaned hard against the door of his lime green Chevy Nova and began jiggering open the lock. The push button mechanism had become stiff lately, and he was babying the old part until he got a chance to soak the striker plate in WD40. If that didn't work, he'd have remove the door panel to repair the latch assembly.

Buddy threw his weight against the car door until it came unstuck and flew open with an ominous scraping sound. He leapt out of the vehicle, steeling himself to face his mom's illness, but couldn't resist casting a parting glance at his beloved muscle car first.

She ain't perfect, but she's still a beauty, Buddy thought as his eyes lingered over the sleek contours of the temperamental sport coupe, his Octane-on-Demand tribute to testosterone. He'd bought the vehicle with his mom's money, which she sent after he'd totaled his old Honda in a nasty fender bender on the parkway.

Buddy paused to rest his hand ceremoniously on the Nova's hard top before sprinting toward the entrance of the sprawling facility. He wasn't exactly a fan of hospitals or nursing homes. The thought of vulnerability and death terrified him. It didn't matter that this particular building was located in a bucolic setting, with aggressively cheerful perennials crowding the flower beds, and what looked like a petting zoo in the adjacent parking lot, mobbed by senior citizens.

The dramatic plantings against a bittersweet backdrop of domesticity reminded Buddy of his father Frank, who was an enthusiastic gardener. While Buddy started self-medicating once Tessie left his dad

120

to be with Garrison, Frank deployed less low-key tactics to cope with the void his ex-wife had left behind.

Young Buddy soon became a captive witness to his father's disintegration. Frank wasn't buoyed by enlightened acceptance, nor could he muster a shred of redeeming dignity. Instead, his suffering over Tessie's betrayal reminded Buddy of the gruesome pictures of leprosy patients he used to pore over secretly in his Nona's medical dictionary. In his father's case, though, it wasn't Frank's nose or other random body parts dropping off; his very soul was festering. As horrible as this affliction was, Buddy couldn't afford to avert his gaze from the emotional wreckage. Instead, he felt compelled to be on guard constantly in case he was needed for damage control.

Vigilance seemed especially crucial when Frank would force Buddy to accompany him on midnight forays to Tessie's new apartment. They'd park, and Frank would shudder and weep. Once he was able to pull himself together, he'd stumble over to his estranged wife's jeep and robotically slash the tires. After the rubber was sufficiently shredded, he'd motion to Buddy, who'd reluctantly retrieve a box of sugar from their car and hand it to his dad. Frank would pour the sugar into Tessie's gas tank and then, as if prompted by some cosmic cue, drive off with Buddy, making forced attempts at casual conversation all the way home.

The next step Frank took post-separation was quitting the plastering business. He'd partnered with Tessie's parents on this venture for years, but had long suspected the paterfamilias was cutting him out of significant revenue streams.

Frank took a new job and was finally able to get some relief driving a McDonald's delivery truck. It was a solitary gig that kept him away from home a lot, especially when he worked the night shift. This was OK with Frank, though, since he couldn't bear spending time with the remnants of his family. His kids had simply become too painful a reminder of Tessie's absence.

Frank figured he could still manage to show his children some affection by dropping off pallets of empty-calorie cuisine at the house—a greasy bonanza of formed and frozen chicken nuggets, along with the piece de resistance—blanched and partially fried potato strips. After all, what's a little arterial trauma if your kids can be eagerly distracted by frequent fast food deliveries?

Frank knew that pining for his ex-wife was a perverse sickness, but he just couldn't purge her toxic charms from his system. Over the years, he'd exhausted every last ounce of his emotional energy just to placate her, until he felt totally gutted. Meanwhile, Tessie continued to feel entitled to it all—unflagging desire, attention, and an obscenely generous clothing allowance.

Eventually, though, Frank found himself remarried to a bipolar stewardess, whose only claim to distinction was putting the family dog down after he'd shed on her velvet, Victorian love seat. Buddy and his sisters were enraged at the loss of their pampered family pet, confronting Frank's bride with such high-decibel hostility that the neighbors called the police. Frank's new wife was so intimidated by his kids' vehement reaction (emotional intelligence wasn't her strong suit) that she convinced him to sell his house and move to Florida, where she suffered UV ray-related cataracts from compulsively admiring their ocean view, promptly followed by terminal heat-stroke.

Left to his own devices once again, Frank sold his Florida home at a loss and drove back to Long Island where, his savings depleted, he had no other recourse but to move in with his sister.

None of this distasteful drama made sense to Buddy. He felt bad for his father, but secretly rooted for his mom, since she was the only one who managed to extract any satisfaction from the crazy, marital mess she and Frank had made. Buddy couldn't help but grudgingly admire her steely talent for shameless self-promotion.

Truth be told, his dad's more exemplary philosophy seemed self-defeating to Buddy. Frank had always strived to do the "right thing" during his marriage and suffered soul-crushing humiliation as a result.

What's the point? Buddy asked himself. *Better to be an unapologetic bitch than a sad-sack saint.*

Buddy had certainly never aspired to sainthood. A decade or so after his parents' divorce, his own wife kicked him out when his grunge band, Hiatal Hernia, failed to rake in significant profits. Feeling disenfranchised, Buddy moved to a garage apartment, where he could play video games and smoke weed in relative concealment. This helped dull the memory of all the money he'd lost (the few shekels left, anyway, after his divorce settlement) when yet another of his ill-advised, day trading runs went south.

15
The Living and the Dead

Buddy made his way down the West Haven Care facility's long, carpeted hallway, which smelled like Pine-Sol® and stewed prunes. Sporadic cries and groans punctuated the monotony as he walked past the residents' doorways. From what he could tell as he passed by, each room contained two beds, a curtain partition and a window. The rooms were spare, but there were personal touches, as well—photos of family gatherings, cheerful greeting card displays, floral arrangements, and the occasional still life in crayon from a precocious grandchild. A handful of visitors, speaking in hushed tones, was scattered among these living quarters, as if sequestered in an archive where vintage people were catalogued and shelved in lieu of rare books.

Buddy stopped for a moment at a busy nursing station, which was manned by the head nurse, a woman of imposing size with an uncompromising gaze.

"I'm looking for my mother's room," Buddy said tentatively. "Can you help me? I... I... think she's here in Unit 2."

"Let's start with her name, young man," the nurse said with exaggerated patience. "That'll make things a lot easier."

Buddy surprised himself by blushing extravagantly, like he used to do as a shy kid who could barely hold a conversation. "Hah… Hand," he stammered. "Her name is Contessa Hand."

"Down the hall and make a left. Room 265." The nurse granted Buddy a tepid smile, waving a meaty hand in the general direction of Tessie's room. Buddy started walking dutifully back down the hall.

"You," an ancient woman shrieked from her wheelchair, parked near the nurse's station. Startled, Buddy stopped short and turned around warily.

"You," the old woman wheezed this time, pointing her long, gnarled finger directly at Buddy. "You're a man. It's a man I'm looking for." Buddy gulped sheepishly.

"Could somebody please come over here and be nice to me already?" The woman seemed hell bent on extracting a response from Buddy, who was already poised to flee the vicinity.

He stopped dead in his tracks, however, upon noticing that several other octogenarian occupants, positioned in wheelchairs nearby, were now staring at him with varying degrees of consciousness. Buddy wasn't keen on being the object of scrutiny, even if most of his audience seemed ready to lapse into a coma. A venerable gentleman in a silk robe leaned on his walker and inched toward Buddy, who felt the old man's rheumy gaze bore straight through him—right down to his core, which Buddy suddenly realized was decidedly gutless.

An officious aide pushed brusquely past Buddy on her way to soothe the shrieking "be nice to me" lady. Grateful for this reprieve, Buddy hurried in the opposite direction until Room 265 came into view.

⋙ 16 ⋘
Happily Ever After

Tact is the ability to tell someone to go to Hell in such a way that they look forward to the trip.

- WINSTON CHURCILL (1874—1965)

Tessie slouched limply in her wheelchair, too spent to move much after her shower. Her memory was slowly improving, but she still couldn't remember the events that brought her to this strange dorm room. She was able to recall, however, what had happened earlier that morning, when some rude women wheeled a large, sling-like contraption into her room.

Talk about the butt crack of dawn, Tessie thought with some bitterness. The women kept talking loudly in a rapid-fire foreign language, as they boosted Tessie from her bed into the scary-looking hammock with a metal frame that hoisted her into the air. There she swayed in an unnatural jackknife position while one of the women passed a cell phone around, prompting raucous laughter from the others.

Must be a picture of the last douchebag she dated. Tessie couldn't help engaging with a good hook-up story, even if her feet were wedged up so high inside the amorphous mesh sling that she almost kicked herself in the face.

Now that was quite the wake-up call, Tessie thought wryly. *I'm not so good at walking or talking anymore, but at least I can still crack myself up.*

A woman wearing a distinctly unflattering hairnet framing her kind face entered the room briskly. "Don't worry, Mommy. I'm your aide, Wanda. Let's

131

get you into your wheelchair and take you for a nice, relaxing shower."

The "nice" shower experience consisted of Tessie sitting stark naked in the middle of a harshly lit bathroom, gripping a chair for dear life as Wanda hosed her down with a biblical torrent of water.

Tessie hoped she wouldn't be forced to relax in the shower on a daily basis. She wondered if this infirmary setting was anything like college housing, but there was a distinct shortage of virile quarterbacks or any other athletic Adonises, for that matter, in her living quarters.

That's gotta be the main benefit of college, right? Sampling a genetic smorgasbord of well-coordinated males. There was one man who'd caught Tessie's eye, but he certainly wasn't up for an impromptu game of touch football. He was older than her usual type, but tall and well-built, nonetheless, with an old money bearing. (Tessie still had a handy knack for spotting men of wealthy lineage.) He walked pretty well for an older guy, and she liked how he stopped by her room most afternoons to present her with a rice pudding from the dining room. Best of all, he didn't irritate Tessie the way her husbands had, since she couldn't remember the gist of their previous conversations once a few hours had elapsed. Short-term memory loss turned out to be a great antidote for the boredom and contempt that Tessie's lovers usually aroused in her after a brief honeymoon period.

Wanda wheeled Tessie out to the hall, once she'd toweled her off and dressed her, parking the wheelchair next to this same, distinguished-looking man, who seemed to be the only person in the center Tessie could tolerate.

"Take good care of her, Garrison," Wanda said warmly, patting him on the shoulder.

"I will," he replied, his face brightening. "She's such a mysterious beauty. I just want to hold her hand and never let go. And she looks so familiar, but I can't place her face. Does that ever happen to you? That maddening sense of déjà vu," he asked Wanda.

"Of course it does, my friend," Wanda responded, laughing. "We all have our senior moments. Maybe it's a blessing. There are definitely a few things I'd like to forget."

Garrison squeezed Tessie's hand and she squeezed back, smiling up at him beatifically.

"You don't talk much, do you, Young Lady?" Garrison asked her affectionately.

Tessie shook her head slowly and smiled some

more. What a relief to let him do all the talking. Just managing her unruly thoughts was hard enough, without having to shoehorn them into coherent sentences.

Just then, Buddy rounded the corner and almost tripped when he saw Tessie and Garrison sitting together in the hall. Tessie was able to recognize her son (*finally, someone familiar*), and slowly raised her hand in his direction. He ran up and enfolded her in a big hug.

"You came," Tessie whispered hoarsely in his ear.

"Of course, Mamacita," Buddy said, fighting back tears. "I came as soon as I heard you were here. The nurses say you can't talk much yet, so I don't want to wear you out. I'll just babble randomly like I normally do, and you can nod your head if you want to."

Tessie beamed at Buddy. The handsome gentleman sitting next to her tried to start conversations all the time, but she just couldn't summon the energy to respond. Besides, he talked more than anyone else she'd ever met. And all those big words he used! She looked forward to bringing him back down to earth, once she felt more like herself again.

"And who do we have here?" Buddy cried, stepping back to take a better look. "Is that you, Garrison? It's been ages since I've seen you."

"You look very familiar, too, Sport," Garrison

134

countered quizzically. "Have we met?"

"Very funny," Buddy laughed. "As if you could ever forget who I am, the guy who keeps hounding you for money. You gotta admit, I've landed myself in an impressive shitload of trouble over the years. I'm addicted to crises! But anyway, it's great to see you guys together—here of all places! Now you can help each other get well again!"

Buddy walked back down the hall on his way out of the building. He felt genuinely moved to see his mom and Garrison holding hands so tenderly. After all these years, their love had actually endured. Even a depressing place like this (not to mention catastrophic blood loss and dementia) couldn't tear them apart.

"See you soon," the head nurse called out as he rushed by. On a whim, Buddy pivoted and walked over to her station.

"I don't even know your name," he said softly, "but I *have* to share this with someone. I've fucked up my life royally these past few years, feeling sorry for myself, abusing drugs and acting like a total dirtbag. I used to despise my stepfather, because he destroyed my family. But now that I've seen him here with my mom—when she needs him most, and they're both so sick—I feel like I owe it to them to turn my life around. I had no idea what love truly meant before today."

"Roxy," the head nurse said gulping, wiping the mist from her eyes. "My name is Roxy. It's a pleasure to meet you."

Buddy grinned, shaking her hand vigorously before heading back toward the parking lot. When he finally sprinted free from the confines of the nursing home, the day burst into view like a festival of sunbeams. As Buddy marveled at the cerulean sky, unmarred by a single cloud, an invigorating breeze stirred, tousling his hair like a lover's first caress.

Made in the USA
Middletown, DE
07 March 2020